TABLE OF CONTENT

Chapter 1: The Institutional Setting .....

Overview of the mental institution as a microcosm of society 1

The role of authority figures in maintaining control 4

Introduction to key characters and their dynamics 8

Chapter 2: The Nature of Madness 13

Exploration of what constitutes sanity vs. insanity 13

The portrayal of mental illness and societal stigma 15

Examining the fine line between conformity and rebellion 20

Chapter 3: The Power of Narration 24

Analysis of Chief Bromden as an unreliable narrator 24

The significance of his perspective on freedom and control 27

Use of symbolism in Chief's hallucinations 31

Chapter 4: Randle McMurphy's Arrival 37

Introduction of McMurphy as a catalyst for change 37

Examination of his rebellious spirit and charisma 40

The initial clash with Nurse Ratched and the establishment 44

Chapter 5: The Struggle for Identity 49

Characters' struggles with their sense of self 49

The impact of the institution on personal identity 52

McMurphy's influence on the patients' sense of agency 57

Chapter 6: The Role of Femininity and Masculinity 60

Analysis of Nurse Ratched's embodiment of patriarchal control...........60

McMurphy's challenge to traditional gender roles 63

The interplay of power dynamics between characters.........................66

Chapter 7: Rebellion and Its Consequences.................................71

Exploration of the various forms of rebellion within the institution 71

The ramifications of McMurphy's defiance 76

Discussion of how rebellion leads to both liberation and repression 80

Chapter 8: The Climax of Conformity 85

Examination of the climax involving McMurphy's fate 85

The ultimate showdown between freedom and control........................88

The emotional and psychological toll on the characters 92

Chapter 9: The Aftermath of Freedom 98

Reflection on the outcomes of the rebellion 98

Chief Bromden's journey towards self-empowerment 102

The lasting impact of McMurphy's legacy on the other patients 106

Chapter 1: The Institutional Setting

Overview of the mental institution as a microcosm of society

Institutional Setting as a Reflection of Society.

This setting serves as a powerful metaphor, encapsulating the various facets of societal norms, hierarchies, and conflicts within its walls. The institution, with its rigid structure and controlled environment, mirrors society's mechanisms of control and conformity.

Structure and Control.

The mental institution's structure is hierarchical, with a clear division between the staff (doctors, nurses, and orderlies) and the patients. This hierarchy reflects the broader societal distinction between those who hold power and those who are subject to it. The institution's rules and routines, designed to maintain order and control, echo the societal norms and laws that govern everyday life. The patients' lack of autonomy and their dependence on the institution's staff highlight the power dynamics that exist in society, where authority figures dictate the terms of existence for those under their control.

Characters as Representations of Societal Roles.

The characters in the mental institution each represent different segments of society and embody various societal roles. The doctors, with their authoritative knowledge and decision-making power, symbolize the educated elite who often dictate the course of societal norms and values. Their interactions with patients reveal underlying biases and assumptions that are prevalent in society, where those in power often impose their perspectives on others.

The nurses and orderlies, positioned between the doctors and the patients, represent the working class. Their role is to implement the doctors' directives and manage the day-to-day operations of the institution. This middle layer reflects the intermediary roles in society, where individuals execute the plans of those in power while also managing the populace. The tension between the nurses and orderlies and the patients highlights the friction that often exists between the working class and the lower classes in society.

Patients as Marginalized Voices.

The patients in the mental institution are the most marginalized voices, much like the underprivileged and oppressed segments of society. Each patient's story and condition reveal different societal issues, such as trauma, neglect, and the consequences of systemic failures. Their confinement within the institution represents the marginalization and exclusion faced by many in society. The institution's attempts to "cure" or "manage" these patients reflect society's efforts to control and suppress dissenting or deviant voices.

Themes of Conformity and Rebellion.

The mental institution enforces strict conformity among its patients, much like society pressures individuals to adhere to established norms. The institution's regimen of medication, therapy, and discipline aims to homogenize the patients' behavior, suppressing individuality and difference. This reflects society's mechanisms of socialization and indoctrination, where deviation from the norm is often met with resistance and punishment.

However, within this setting, there are also sparks of rebellion. Some patients resist the institution's control, seeking to assert their identity and autonomy. This resistance parallels societal movements and individuals who challenge the status quo, advocating for change and greater freedom. The tension between conformity and rebellion within the institution mirrors the ongoing struggle between societal control and individual freedom in the broader context.

Societal Critique Through the Institution.

The mental institution in Chapter 1 serves as a critique of societal structures and norms. By portraying the institution's flaws and the suffering of its patients, the narrative highlights the inadequacies and injustices within society. The patients' stories underscore the impact of systemic issues such as poverty, discrimination, and lack of access to adequate mental health care. This critique encourages readers to reflect on how societal structures and norms contribute to the marginalization and suffering of individuals.

Character Development and Interaction.

The interactions between characters within the mental institution provide deeper insights into societal dynamics. The relationships between doctors and patients, nurses and orderlies, and among the patients themselves reveal the complexities of power, empathy, and conflict that exist in society. These interactions highlight how individuals navigate their roles and identities within a hierarchical system, often struggling to maintain their sense of self amidst external pressures.

The characters and their interactions within this setting provide a rich tapestry for exploring broader societal themes. Through the detailed portrayal of the institution, the narrative invites readers to examine the ways in which societal norms and power structures shape individual lives and experiences. This analysis of the institutional setting as a microcosm of society offers a profound commentary on the human condition and the societal forces that influence it.

The role of authority figures in maintaining control

This chapter sets the stage for the broader exploration of power dynamics, control, and resistance within an institutional framework. By examining the interactions between authority figures and the individuals they oversee, we gain insights into the mechanisms of power and the subtle ways in which control is exerted and resisted.

The institutional setting is depicted as a microcosm of society, where hierarchical structures and authority figures play a critical role in maintaining order and control. This environment is characterized by strict rules, surveillance, and a clear delineation of power. The authority figures, including administrators, supervisors, and security personnel, are instrumental in enforcing these rules and ensuring compliance among the inmates or members of the institution.

Authority Figures and Their Methods of Control.

The authority figures in this chapter are portrayed as both omnipresent and omnipotent, embodying the institution's power. Their methods of control are multifaceted, encompassing both overt and covert strategies.

Surveillance and Monitoring.

One of the primary tools used by authority figures to maintain control is surveillance. The institution is depicted as a panopticon, where inmates are constantly watched and monitored. This creates a sense of perpetual visibility, which in turn fosters self-regulation and compliance. The authority figures leverage this surveillance to preempt any potential disruptions to the institutional order.

Enforcement of Rules and Punishments.

The authority figures also maintain control through the strict enforcement of rules and the meting out of punishments. Any deviation from the established norms is swiftly addressed, often with severe consequences. This punitive approach serves as a deterrent, reinforcing the institution's authority and discouraging dissent.

Psychological Manipulation.

Beyond physical surveillance and punishment, authority figures also employ psychological manipulation to maintain control. They cultivate an atmosphere of fear and uncertainty, where the boundaries of acceptable behavior are deliberately blurred. This psychological warfare destabilizes the inmates, making them more pliable and easier to control.

Character Development and Interactions with Authority Figures.

The interactions between the inmates and authority figures are pivotal in shaping the narrative and character development. These interactions reveal the complex dynamics of power and resistance, and how authority figures influence the inmates' behavior and psyche.

Protagonist's Struggle with Authority.

The protagonist, often depicted as a figure of resistance, embodies the tension between individual autonomy and institutional control. Their interactions with authority figures are marked by defiance and resilience, highlighting their struggle to maintain a sense of self amidst oppressive control.

The protagonist's journey is one of both external and internal conflict. Externally, they confront the authority figures directly, challenging their legitimacy and power. Internally, they grapple with the psychological toll of institutionalization, questioning their own identity and values. This dual struggle underscores the profound impact of authority figures on the protagonist's character development.

Supporting Characters and Their Responses to Authority.

Supporting characters offer a diverse range of responses to authority, reflecting the varying degrees of compliance and resistance within the institution. Some characters, worn down by the relentless control, exhibit a resigned acceptance of their fate. Others, however, display subtle acts of defiance, seeking to carve out spaces of autonomy within the confines of the institution.

These varied responses enrich the narrative, illustrating the complex interplay between authority and resistance. They also serve to humanize the inmates, revealing the personal costs of institutional control and the resilience of the human spirit.

The Authority Figures' Perspective.

While the narrative primarily focuses on the inmates' experiences, occasional glimpses into the perspective of the authority figures provide a more nuanced understanding of their role in maintaining control.

The Burden of Authority.

Authority figures are often portrayed as individuals burdened by the responsibilities of their role. They are tasked with maintaining order and ensuring the smooth functioning of the institution, a daunting challenge given the inherent tensions and conflicts within such a setting. This burden can lead to a dehumanizing detachment, where authority figures become desensitized to the suffering of those they oversee.

Moral Ambiguity and Ethical Dilemmas.

The authority figures also grapple with moral ambiguity and ethical dilemmas. Their actions, while aimed at maintaining control, often raise questions about the nature of justice and the limits of authority. This moral complexity adds depth to their characters, challenging readers to consider the broader implications of institutional power.

Thematic Exploration of Control and Resistance.

The theme of control and resistance is central to the narrative of Chapter 1. The authority figures' strategies and the inmates' responses collectively explore the dynamics of power within the institutional setting.

The Illusion of Control.

Despite the authority figures' efforts to maintain control, the narrative suggests that true control is an illusion. The inmates' acts of resistance, whether overt or covert, reveal the inherent limitations of institutional power. This theme underscores the fragility of authority and the indomitable human spirit.

The Cycle of Oppression.

The chapter also explores the cyclical nature of oppression and resistance. Authority figures' attempts to suppress dissent often lead to further resistance, creating a perpetual cycle of control and defiance. This cycle highlights the systemic nature of institutional power and the challenges of achieving lasting change.

Through detailed character development and intricate plot dynamics, the chapter delves into the mechanisms of power, the complexities of resistance, and the moral ambiguities inherent in authority. The interactions between authority figures and inmates serve as a lens through which the broader themes of control and defiance are examined, offering a nuanced and insightful commentary on the nature of power and its impact on individuals.

Introduction to key characters and their dynamics

This chapter serves as a foundational blueprint, setting the stage for the intricate interplay of personalities and motivations that will drive the narrative forward.

Key Characters and Their Initial Dynamics.

1. The Protagonist: Alex Delgado.

Alex Delgado is introduced as a resilient and ambitious young professional, newly appointed to a pivotal role within the institution. From the outset, Alex's character is depicted as a blend of idealism and pragmatism. His background, hinted at with subtle strokes, suggests a history of overcoming adversity, which has steeled his resolve and shaped his work ethic. Alex's primary motivation is to effect meaningful change within the institution, and his initial interactions are marked by a keen sense of observation and a strategic approach to understanding the institutional landscape.

2. The Mentor: Dr. Evelyn Grant.

Dr. Evelyn Grant, a seasoned veteran with decades of experience, is portrayed as the mentor figure to Alex. Her character exudes wisdom and authority, tempered by a deep-seated commitment to the institution's values. Dr. Grant's role is critical in shaping Alex's journey, as she provides him with invaluable insights and guidance. The dynamic between Alex and Dr. Grant is characterized by mutual respect, though it is evident that their relationship will be tested by differing perspectives on institutional change. Dr. Grant's initial advice to Alex is laden with caution, emphasizing the importance of patience and diplomacy in navigating the complex institutional politics.

3. The Antagonist: Victor Kane.

Victor Kane emerges as the primary antagonist, a formidable figure whose authority within the institution is both respected and feared. Victor's introduction is laced with an aura of intimidation; his presence commands the room, and his words carry an undercurrent of threat. His opposition to Alex's progressive ideas is immediate and staunch, rooted in a belief in maintaining the status quo. Victor's character is complex, driven by a mixture of genuine concern for the institution's stability and a personal stake in preserving his power. The tension between Victor and Alex is palpable from their first encounter, setting up a classic conflict between innovation and tradition.

4. The Ally: Sarah Ramirez.

Sarah Ramirez, a colleague of Alex, is introduced as a potential ally and confidante. Her character is warm and approachable, providing a stark contrast to the often cold and calculating institutional environment. Sarah's background in the institution equips her with insider knowledge, which she shares with Alex, aiding him in understanding the unwritten rules and power dynamics at play. The camaraderie between Alex and Sarah is immediate, grounded in shared values and a mutual desire to see positive change. However, Sarah's cautious nature hints at potential conflicts, as she understands the risks involved in challenging the institutional hierarchy.

5. The Bureaucrats: The Board of Directors.

The Board of Directors is introduced as a collective character, representing the entrenched bureaucracy of the institution. Their interactions with Alex are formal and guarded, reflecting the institution's resistance to change. The dynamics between Alex and the Board are characterized by a push-and-pull of innovation versus tradition. The Board's skepticism towards Alex's proposals is evident, and their initial interactions are marked by a careful dance of diplomacy and assertiveness on Alex's part.

Character Dynamics and Interactions.

The dynamics between these key characters are central to the unfolding plot in Chapter 1. The narrative deftly weaves together their interactions, establishing a complex web of relationships that will drive the story forward.

1. Alex and Dr. Grant: Mentorship and Conflict.

The relationship between Alex and Dr. Grant is one of the most significant dynamics in the chapter. Dr. Grant's mentorship is crucial for Alex's development, providing him with the wisdom and perspective needed to navigate the institution. However, their differing approaches to change—Alex's impatience versus Dr. Grant's caution—foreshadow potential conflicts. This dynamic tension is a driving force in the narrative, highlighting the generational and philosophical divide within the institution.

2. Alex and Victor: The Central Conflict.

The antagonism between Alex and Victor Kane is the central conflict of the chapter. Victor's resistance to Alex's ideas sets up a classic battle of wills. Victor's character, with his deep-seated belief in the institution's traditional values, represents a significant obstacle to Alex's vision. This conflict is not just ideological but also personal, as Victor perceives Alex's innovations as a direct threat to his authority and legacy.

3. Alex and Sarah: Collaboration and Caution.

The relationship between Alex and Sarah is marked by collaboration and mutual support. Sarah's insider knowledge and cautious approach complement Alex's bold vision, creating a balanced partnership. However, Sarah's awareness of the risks involved in challenging the institution's hierarchy introduces an element of tension. Her character serves as a voice of reason, reminding Alex of the potential consequences of his actions.

4. Alex and the Board: Diplomacy and Resistance.

The interactions between Alex and the Board of Directors highlight the institutional resistance to change. The Board's skepticism and guarded demeanor force Alex to refine his approach, balancing assertiveness with diplomacy. This dynamic underscores the broader theme of innovation struggling against entrenched bureaucracy, a recurring motif in the narrative.

Plot Development and Thematic Underpinnings.

The plot development in Chapter 1 is intricately tied to the introduction of these key characters and their dynamics. Alex's journey is set against the backdrop of an institution resistant to change, with each character representing different facets of this resistance. The initial interactions and conflicts lay the groundwork for the central themes of the story: the struggle for innovation, the tension between tradition and progress, and the personal costs of institutional change.

1. Innovation vs. Tradition.

The clash between Alex's innovative ideas and the institution's traditional values is a central theme. Alex's character embodies the drive for progress, while Victor Kane and the Board represent the weight of tradition. This theme is explored through their interactions, highlighting the challenges of implementing change in a conservative environment.

2. Mentorship and Growth.

The mentorship dynamic between Alex and Dr. Grant adds depth to the narrative, illustrating the importance of guidance and wisdom in personal and professional growth. Their relationship is a microcosm of the broader institutional dynamics, reflecting the tension between experience and innovation.

3. Power and Authority.

The theme of power and authority is woven throughout the chapter, with Victor Kane's character serving as a focal point. Victor's resistance to Alex's ideas is not just about institutional stability but also about maintaining his own power. This theme explores the complexities of authority and the personal stakes involved in wielding it.

4. Collaboration and Caution.

The partnership between Alex and Sarah introduces the theme of collaboration tempered by caution. Sarah's character provides a necessary counterbalance to Alex's boldness, emphasizing the need for strategic thinking in the face of institutional resistance.

The intricate interplay of personalities and motivations sets the stage for a compelling narrative, rich with thematic depth and character-driven conflict. The relationships between Alex, Dr. Grant, Victor Kane, Sarah Ramirez, and the Board of Directors are meticulously crafted, laying the foundation for a story that explores the complexities of institutional change and the human elements that drive it.

Chapter 2: The Nature of Madness

Exploration of what constitutes sanity vs. insanity

Through the development of its characters and the unfolding of the plot, the chapter challenges conventional notions of mental health, blurring the lines between what is considered sane and insane.

The chapter opens with the protagonist, Dr. Evelyn Grant, a renowned psychiatrist, facing a moral and professional dilemma. Her patient, Samuel Blake, is a complex character whose behavior defies easy categorization. Samuel exhibits symptoms that align with several psychiatric disorders, yet he also displays moments of profound clarity and insight that challenge Dr. Grant's understanding of his condition. This duality sets the stage for a nuanced exploration of the nature of madness.

Dr. Grant's initial assessment of Samuel is rooted in traditional psychiatric practices. She meticulously documents his erratic behavior, delusional thoughts, and periods of dissociation. These symptoms are textbook examples of severe mental illness, leading her to prescribe a rigorous treatment plan that includes medication and intensive therapy. However, as the narrative progresses, Dr. Grant begins to question the efficacy and ethics of her approach. Samuel's moments of lucidity, where he articulates coherent and insightful thoughts about his condition and the world around him, force her to reconsider the binary classification of sanity and insanity.

The plot takes a significant turn when Dr. Grant decides to employ a more holistic approach to understanding Samuel's condition. She delves into his personal history, uncovering traumatic experiences that have shaped his psyche. This investigation reveals that Samuel's "madness" may be a coping mechanism, a way for his mind to process and protect itself from past traumas. This revelation prompts Dr. Grant to explore alternative therapeutic methods, including art therapy and narrative therapy, which allow Samuel to express and process his experiences in a non-linear, non-verbal manner.

Samuel's character development is central to the exploration of sanity versus insanity. Initially portrayed as a deeply troubled individual, his layers are gradually peeled back to reveal a multifaceted personality. His moments of lucidity are not mere anomalies but windows into a complex inner world. Samuel's insights into his condition, his awareness of his fragmented self, and his ability to articulate these experiences challenge the stereotype of the "insane" individual as someone devoid of self-awareness or rationality.

The narrative also introduces secondary characters whose perspectives on sanity and insanity further complicate the theme. Dr. Grant's mentor, Dr. Raymond Clarke, represents the old guard of psychiatry, steadfast in his belief in the rigid boundaries between sanity and madness. His interactions with Dr. Grant serve as a foil to her evolving understanding, highlighting the generational and ideological divide within the field of mental health.

Another pivotal character is Emma, Samuel's sister, who provides a deeply personal and empathetic perspective. Emma's relationship with Samuel is fraught with complexity; she oscillates between frustration and deep love for her brother. Her journey mirrors Dr. Grant's in many ways, as she too must navigate the murky waters of what it means to be sane or insane. Emma's unwavering support for Samuel, despite his erratic behavior, underscores the theme that love and empathy can transcend traditional boundaries of mental health.

The climax of the chapter occurs during a groundbreaking therapy session where Samuel, guided by Dr. Grant, experiences a breakthrough. Through a combination of guided imagery and narrative therapy, Samuel confronts the traumatic memories that have long haunted him. This cathartic experience does not "cure" him in the traditional sense, but it allows him to integrate these fragmented parts of himself into a more cohesive identity. This moment is pivotal as it blurs the lines between sanity and insanity, suggesting that mental health exists on a spectrum rather than in binary terms.

The chapter concludes with Dr. Grant reflecting on the implications of her work with Samuel. She grapples with the realization that the traditional psychiatric paradigm may be inadequate in capturing the complexity of humanExperience. Her journey with Samuel leads her to advocate for a more flexible, empathetic approach to mental health, one that recognizes the fluidity of the human psyche and the profound impact of personal history on mental well-being.

Through the intricate development of its characters and the unfolding of its plot, the chapter challenges conventional psychiatric paradigms and advocates for a more nuanced understanding of mental health. Dr. Grant's evolving perspective, Samuel's complex character, and the empathetic portrayal of mental illness collectively underscore the theme that sanity and insanity are not fixed states but exist on a dynamic and deeply personal spectrum.

The portrayal of mental illness and societal stigma

The Protagonist's Journey.

The protagonist, Alex, is introduced as a successful professional who grapples with severe anxiety and depression. I meticulously describes Alex's internal struggle, painting a vivid picture of the debilitating effects of these conditions. Alex's journey is marked by moments of intense panic attacks, profound sadness, and a sense of isolation. The narrative technique of internal monologue is used effectively to provide readers with a deep understanding of Alex's thoughts and feelings.

Alex's character development is central to the chapter's exploration of mental illness. Initially, Alex attempts to conceal his struggles from colleagues and friends, fearing judgment and professional repercussions. This fear is rooted in the societal stigma that equates mental illness with weakness or incompetence. As the chapter progresses, Alex's facade begins to crumble, leading to a pivotal moment where he seeks professional help. This decision marks a turning point, not only for Alex but also for the narrative's trajectory, highlighting the importance of acknowledging and addressing mental health issues.

Supporting Characters and Their Perspectives.

Several supporting characters play crucial roles in illustrating different aspects of societal stigma. Emily, Alex's colleague and confidante, represents a more empathetic view. Her character is portrayed as understanding and supportive, challenging the stereotype that mental illness is something to be hidden or ashamed of. Through Emily, i emphasizes the importance of a supportive environment in the healing process.

In contrast, characters like Michael, Alex's boss, embody the harsh reality of workplace stigma. Michael's dismissive attitude towards Alex's struggles reflects a common societal view that mental health issues are a sign of personal failing rather than legitimate medical conditions. This portrayal serves to underscore the damaging impact of such attitudes on individuals who are already vulnerable.

The Antagonist's Role.

The antagonist, Dr. Roberts, is a complex character who initially appears to be a source of support for Alex. However, as the story unfolds, it becomes clear that Dr. Roberts represents the medicalization of mental illness. His approach to treatment is mechanistic and lacks empathy, focusing more on medication and less on understanding Alex's experiences. This portrayal raises critical questions about the healthcare system's approach to mental illness and the potential for dehumanization in clinical settings.

Thematic Exploration.

Mental Illness as a Personal Struggle.

The chapter delves deeply into the personal struggle of living with mental illness. Alex's experiences are depicted with raw honesty, highlighting the daily challenges and the pervasive sense of hopelessness that can accompany conditions like anxiety and depression. The author's use of descriptive language allows readers to feel the weight of Alex's experiences, fostering empathy and understanding.

Societal Stigma and Misconceptions.

Societal stigma is a recurring theme throughout the chapter. The narrative explores how misconceptions about mental illness contribute to the marginalization of those affected. I uses various characters and scenarios to illustrate the different forms that stigma can take, from overt discrimination to more subtle forms of bias.

For example, Alex's fear of disclosing his condition at work is a direct result of the stigma that equates mental illness with unreliability or incompetence. This fear is validated when Michael reacts negatively to Alex's struggles, reinforcing the idea that mental health issues are best kept hidden. Through these interactions, i critiques societal attitudes and calls for greater awareness and acceptance.

The Role of Empathy and Support.

Empathy and support are portrayed as crucial elements in addressing mental illness. Emily's character exemplifies the positive impact of a supportive and understanding environment. Her willingness to listen and offer support without judgment helps Alex feel less isolated and more hopeful. This dynamic highlights the importance of empathy in combating the isolation that often accompanies mental illness.

The Critique of the Medical System.

Dr. Roberts' character serves as a critique of the medical system's approach to mental illness. His mechanistic approach and lack of empathy highlight the pitfalls of reducing mental health to purely biological terms. This portrayal raises important questions about the need for a more holistic and compassionate approach to mental health care, one that considers the individual's experiences and personal context.

Narrative Techniques.

Descriptive Language and Imagery.

I employs rich descriptive language and vivid imagery to convey the characters' experiences and emotions. This technique is particularly effective in portraying Alex's internal world, allowing readers to gain a deep understanding of his struggles. The use of metaphors and similes to describe Alex's anxiety and depression helps to make these abstract concepts more tangible and relatable.

Internal Monologue.

The extensive use of internal monologue provides insight into the characters' thoughts and feelings, particularly Alex's. This narrative technique allows readers to experience Alex's journey from his perspective, fostering a sense of intimacy and empathy. The internal monologue also serves to highlight the contrast between Alex's internal struggles and his external facade, underscoring the theme of societal stigma.

Dialogue.

Dialogue is used effectively to reveal the attitudes and beliefs of different characters. Conversations between Alex and other characters, such as Emily and Michael, provide a platform for exploring different viewpoints on mental illness. The contrasting dialogues between empathetic and dismissive characters serve to highlight the spectrum of societal attitudes towards mental health.

Critical Analysis.

Strengths.

The chapter excels in its nuanced portrayal of mental illness and societal stigma. The author's ability to create complex, multifaceted characters adds depth to the narrative, making the exploration of these themes more impactful. The use of descriptive language and internal monologue enhances the reader's understanding and empathy, making the story both engaging and thought-provoking.

Weaknesses.

One potential weakness is the portrayal of Dr. Roberts, which could be seen as overly critical of the medical profession. While the critique of the mechanistic approach to mental health care is valid, a more balanced representation might have included a character who embodies a more holistic and empathetic approach within the medical field.

Impact.

The chapter has a significant impact on the reader, challenging preconceived notions about mental illness and encouraging a more compassionate and informed perspective. By humanizing the experience of mental illness and exposing the damaging effects of societal stigma, i fosters a greater sense of empathy and understanding.

Chapter 2 of "The Nature of Madness" offers a profound exploration of mental illness and societal stigma, using well-developed characters and a compelling narrative to highlight these themes. The author's insightful portrayal of Alex's journey, coupled with the contrasting perspectives of supporting characters, provides a multifaceted view of the challenges faced by those with mental health issues. The chapter's critical examination of societal attitudes and the medical system's approach to mental illness invites readers to reflect on their own beliefs and consider the importance of empathy and support in addressing mental health challenges. Through its rich descriptive language, nuanced character development, and thought-provoking themes, this chapter sets the stage for a deeper exploration of the nature of madness and the potential for healing and understanding.

Examining the fine line between conformity and rebellion

This chapter delves into the protagonists' struggle to maintain their individuality while navigating societal expectations, revealing the complex interplay between conformity and rebellion.

Plot Analysis: The Struggle for Identity.

The chapter opens with the protagonist, Dr. Emily Clarke, a renowned psychologist, facing a moral dilemma. She is tasked with evaluating a patient, Daniel Archer, who is accused of a violent crime. The authorities and her colleagues are convinced of Daniel's guilt, but Emily's initial interactions with him leave her questioning the narrative presented to her. This sets the stage for an exploration of conformity and rebellion within the context of professional ethics and personal beliefs.

As Emily delves deeper into Daniel's case, she discovers inconsistencies in the evidence and a history of mental illness that could explain his behavior. Her superiors, however, pressure her to align with the prevailing opinion and declare Daniel mentally competent to stand trial. This external pressure highlights the conflict between conformity—adhering to the expectations of her profession and society—and rebellion—challenging the status quo to seek the truth.

Emily's internal struggle is further complicated by her past experiences. She had previously faced backlash for questioning established norms in a high-profile case, which led to her temporary ostracization from the professional community. This backstory adds depth to her character, illustrating the personal and professional risks involved in defying conformity. Her reluctance to relive that experience creates a palpable tension as she weighs the consequences of her decisions.

Character Development: The Protagonist's Journey.

Dr. Emily Clarke's character arc in Chapter 2 is a profound exploration of the fine line between conformity and rebellion. Initially portrayed as a diligent and respected professional, Emily's commitment to her patients and ethical standards is evident. However, as the chapter progresses, her interactions with Daniel and the mounting pressure from her colleagues force her to confront her own beliefs and values.

Emily's evolving perspective on Daniel's case mirrors her internal conflict. She oscillates between the desire to conform to the expectations of her role and the urge to rebel against what she perceives as an unjust system. This duality is brilliantly depicted through her internal monologues and interactions with other characters, showcasing her vulnerability and strength.

A pivotal moment in Emily's development occurs when she uncovers a crucial piece of evidence that supports Daniel's innocence. This discovery galvanizes her resolve to pursue the truth, despite the potential repercussions. Her decision to stand by Daniel, even at the risk of her career, marks a significant turning point. It underscores her transition from passive conformity to active rebellion, driven by a deep-seated conviction in justice and moral integrity.

Supporting Characters: Catalysts for Conflict and Growth.

The supporting characters in Chapter 2 play crucial roles in highlighting the theme of conformity versus rebellion. Dr. Robert Hathaway, Emily's mentor and a staunch advocate of the institution's practices, represents the embodiment of conformity. His unwavering belief in the system and dismissal of Emily's concerns serve as a constant reminder of the pressures she faces.

Conversely, Sarah Mitchell, a fellow psychologist and Emily's confidante, embodies the spirit of rebellion. Sarah's encouragement and support bolster Emily's resolve, providing a counterbalance to the oppressive conformity advocated by Dr. Hathaway and others. Sarah's character is instrumental in Emily's journey, offering a voice of reason and solidarity that empowers Emily to take a stand.

Daniel Archer, the patient at the center of the controversy, also plays a significant role in Emily's development. His enigmatic personality and the ambiguity surrounding his mental state challenge Emily's preconceptions. As she grows more invested in his case, Daniel becomes a catalyst for her rebellion against the rigid structures of her profession. His plight humanizes the abstract concept of rebellion, making Emily's struggle more tangible and emotionally resonant.

Thematic Exploration: Conformity vs. Rebellion.

The theme of conformity versus rebellion is central to Chapter 2, manifesting in various forms throughout the narrative. The institutional setting of the psychiatric facility symbolizes the rigid structures that demand conformity. The pressure to conform is not merely external but also internalized by the characters, influencing their decisions and interactions.

Emily's journey reflects the broader societal struggle between adhering to established norms and challenging them. The narrative explores the psychological and emotional toll of this conflict, highlighting the courage required to rebel against ingrained systems. Emily's eventual decision to support Daniel, despite the risks, serves as a powerful testament to the importance of individuality and moral integrity.

The fine line between conformity and rebellion is also depicted through the nuanced portrayal of mental illness. Daniel's character challenges the conventional understanding of madness, prompting Emily and the readers to question the labels and judgments imposed by society.

This subversion of expectations underscores the complexity of the human psyche and the dangers of simplistic categorizations.

Chapter 2 of "The Nature of Madness" masterfully examines the fine line between conformity and rebellion, using the characters' journeys to explore the broader implications of these themes. Emily's evolution from a conformist professional to a rebellious advocate for justice encapsulates the narrative's core message: the importance of questioning societal norms and standing up for one's beliefs, even in the face of adversity.

The chapter's exploration of conformity and rebellion extends beyond individual characters to critique societal institutions and their impact on personal freedom and ethical decision-making. By delving into the psychological and emotional dimensions of this conflict, the narrative offers a compelling and thought-provoking analysis of what it means to conform and rebel in the modern world.

Through its intricate plot, well-developed characters, and thematic depth, the chapter offers valuable insights into the complexities of human behavior and the enduring struggle for individuality and justice.

Chapter 3: The Power of Narration

Analysis of Chief Bromden as an unreliable narrator

In Ken Kesey's "One Flew Over the Cuckoo's Nest," Chief Bromden serves as the novel's narrator, offering a unique and often unreliable perspective on the events within the psychiatric hospital. This unreliability is particularly evident in Chapter 3, where Bromden's narrative reveals much about his own mental state and the power dynamics within the institution. By examining Bromden's narrative style, his perceptions of reality, and his interactions with other characters, we can gain a deeper understanding of how Kesey uses Bromden's unreliability to enhance the novel's themes and character development.

Bromden's Narrative Style.

Bromden's narrative is characterized by a blend of vivid, hallucinatory imagery and fragmented, disjointed thoughts. This style immediately signals to the reader that Bromden's perception of reality is distorted. McMurphy with a mixture of fear, awe, and confusion. His descriptions often veer into the surreal, reflecting his own mental instability. For instance, Bromden's depiction of the hospital's machinery as a living, malevolent entity underscores his paranoia and his sense of being oppressed by an all-powerful, mechanical force.

This narrative style serves several purposes. Firstly, it draws the reader into Bromden's subjective experience, making his fear and confusion palpable. Secondly, it creates a sense of ambiguity about the events being described. Because Bromden's perceptions are unreliable, the reader is constantly questioning the veracity of his account. This narrative strategy heightens the novel's tension and suspense, as the reader must navigate Bromden's distorted reality to uncover the truth.

Perception of Reality.

Bromden's unreliability is further emphasized by his frequent hallucinations and delusions. This fog is a recurring motif in Bromden's narrative, symbolizing his sense of disorientation and his desire to retreat from reality. When McMurphy arrives, Bromden perceives him as a disruptive, almost mythic figure who challenges the hospital's authority and the rigid order imposed by Nurse Ratched.

Bromden's perception of McMurphy is particularly significant. He sees McMurphy as a liberator, a figure who can break through the fog and bring clarity to the patients' lives. However, Bromden's idealization of McMurphy is tinged with his own desires and projections. McMurphy represents the strength and freedom that Bromden feels he lacks, and thus, Bromden's portrayal of him is colored by his own longing for empowerment. This idealization highlights Bromden's unreliability, as it reveals his tendency to project his own needs and fantasies onto the people around him.

Interactions with Other Characters.

Bromden's interactions with other characters in Chapter 3 further illustrate his unreliability. His relationship with Nurse Ratched, the hospital's authoritarian figure, is particularly telling. Bromden describes Nurse Ratched with a mixture of fear and resentment, portraying her as a cold, calculating manipulator who exerts control over the patients through psychological manipulation and intimidation. This portrayal is influenced by Bromden's own feelings of powerlessness and his deep-seated fear of authority.

Additionally, Bromden's interactions with the other patients reveal his status as an outsider within the hospital. He often feels invisible and ignored by both the staff and his fellow patients, a feeling that contributes to his sense of isolation and his unreliable narration. Bromden's sense of invisibility is both literal and metaphorical; he often feels that he can disappear into the background, unnoticed by those around him. This sense of invisibility is compounded by his self-imposed silence; Bromden rarely speaks, and when he does, his words are often dismissed or ignored.

Impact on Character Development.

Bromden's unreliability significantly impacts the development of both his character and the novel's other characters. His distorted perceptions and fragmented narrative create a complex, multi-layered portrait of life within the psychiatric hospital. By presenting events through Bromden's eyes, Kesey allows the reader to experience the hospital's oppressive atmosphere firsthand, making the novel's critique of institutional power more immediate and visceral.

Moreover, Bromden's unreliability serves as a commentary on the nature of truth and perception. His narrative challenges the notion of a single, objective reality, suggesting instead that truth is subjective and shaped by individual experiences and mental states. This theme is central to the novel, as Kesey explores the ways in which institutional power and societal norms shape and distort individual identities.

Thematic Implications.

Kesey uses Bromden's unreliability to explore several key themes in "One Flew Over the Cuckoo's Nest. " One of the most prominent themes is the conflict between individuality and conformity. Bromden's fragmented narrative and distorted perceptions reflect his struggle to maintain his identity in the face of institutional pressures to conform. His hallucinations and delusions can be seen as attempts to escape the oppressive reality of the hospital, highlighting the toll that conformity takes on the human psyche.

Another important theme is the power dynamics between the oppressed and the oppressors. Bromden's portrayal of Nurse Ratched and the hospital staff underscores the novel's critique of authoritarianism and the abuse of power. By presenting the hospital as a microcosm of society, Kesey critiques the ways in which power is wielded to control and suppress individuals. Bromden's narrative, with its emphasis on fear and oppression, serves as a powerful indictment of these dynamics.

His narrative style, marked by vivid hallucinations and fragmented thoughts, reflects his own mental instability and creates a sense of ambiguity about the events being described. Bromden's interactions with other characters and his distorted perceptions of reality further emphasize his unreliability, highlighting the subjective nature of truth and the impact of institutional power on individual identity. Through Bromden's eyes, Kesey crafts a powerful critique of conformity, authority, and the human spirit's resilience in the face of oppression.

The significance of his perspective on freedom and control

The Protagonist's Journey.

The protagonist, whose name is revealed to be Alexander, has been on a tumultuous journey of self-discovery. By Chapter 3, he has encountered numerous challenges that have tested his resilience and forced him to confront his deepest fears. His perspective on freedom and control is not static; it evolves as he navigates through the complexities of his world.

Early Encounters with Freedom and Control.

At the beginning of the story, Alexander's understanding of freedom is simplistic. He equates freedom with physical liberty, a life without constraints or obligations. This naive view is quickly challenged when he is thrust into a situation where his freedom is severely restricted. The narrative cleverly juxtaposes his initial perception with the harsh realities he faces, making him question the true nature of freedom.

Elias introduces him to the idea that true freedom is not merely the absence of physical constraints but the ability to make choices that align with one's values and beliefs. This philosophical discourse marks a turning point in Alexander's understanding of freedom. He begins to realize that control, in the form of self-discipline and determination, is essential for achieving true freedom.

The Role of Narration in Shaping Perspective.

The power of narration in shaping Alexander's perspective cannot be overstated. The narrative voice provides a lens through which readers interpret Alexander's thoughts and actions. This shift allows readers to delve deeper into Alexander's psyche, understanding his internal struggles and the evolution of his thoughts on freedom and control.

Alexander's Internal Monologue.

Alexander's internal monologue in Chapter 3 is rich with introspection. He reflects on his past experiences, questioning the choices he has made and the lessons he has learned. This introspection is crucial for his development as a character. Through his thoughts, the readers see a shift from a reactive to a proactive mindset. He begins to understand that while external forces may impose limitations, his response to these forces is within his control.

The narration captures Alexander's struggle to reconcile his desire for freedom with the necessity of control. He grapples with the idea that true freedom requires a degree of self-control and discipline. This internal conflict is a central theme of the chapter, highlighting the complexity of the protagonist's journey.

Interactions with Other Characters.

Alexander's interactions with other characters in Chapter 3 further illuminate his evolving perspective on freedom and control. Each character he encounters serves as a foil, reflecting different aspects of his internal struggle.

The Mentor: Elias.

Elias plays a crucial role in Alexander's development. As a mentor, he challenges Alexander's preconceived notions and pushes him to think critically about his beliefs. Their dialogues are filled with philosophical debates about the nature of freedom and the role of control in achieving it. Elias's wisdom and guidance help Alexander see that freedom is not an end in itself but a means to live a life of purpose and integrity.

The Antagonist: Victor.

Victor, the antagonist, represents the extreme of control without freedom. His character is a stark contrast to Alexander's evolving ideology. Victor's ruthless pursuit of power at the expense of personal freedom highlights the dangers of an imbalanced perspective. Through their confrontations, Alexander learns the importance of maintaining a balance between freedom and control. Victor's downfall serves as a cautionary tale, reinforcing the narrative's message about the perils of unchecked control.

The Love Interest: Isabella.

Isabella, Alexander's love interest, embodies the ideal of harmonious coexistence between freedom and control. Her character is portrayed as someone who has found a balance between pursuing her passions and adhering to her principles. Isabella's influence on Alexander is subtle yet profound. Through their relationship, Alexander begins to see the beauty of a life where freedom and control are not opposing forces but complementary aspects of a fulfilling existence.

Symbolism and Themes.

Chapter 3 is rich with symbolism that reinforces the themes of freedom and control. I uses various literary devices to deepen the readers' understanding of these concepts.

The Labyrinth.

One of the most potent symbols in Chapter 3 is the labyrinth. The labyrinth represents the complexities of life and the journey towards self-discovery. As Alexander navigates through the labyrinth, he encounters various obstacles that test his resolve and force him to make difficult decisions. Each turn in the labyrinth symbolizes a choice, highlighting the interplay between freedom and control. The labyrinth is not just a physical space but a metaphor for the internal journey Alexander undertakes.

The Key.

The key is another significant symbol in the chapter. It represents the potential for unlocking true freedom. However, the key is not handed to Alexander; he must earn it through his actions and choices. This symbolizes the idea that freedom is not a given but something that must be actively pursued and maintained through control and discipline.

Plot Development.

The plot of Chapter 3 is intricately woven around Alexander's evolving perspective on freedom and control. Each event and encounter is carefully crafted to contribute to his development as a character.

The Trial.

A pivotal moment in the chapter is Alexander's trial. This trial is not a legal proceeding but a metaphorical test of his character. He is faced with a series of moral dilemmas that force him to confront his beliefs about freedom and control. The trial serves as a crucible, refining his understanding and strengthening his resolve. By the end of the trial,

Alexander emerges with a clearer sense of purpose and a deeper understanding of the balance between freedom and control.

The Revelation.

The climax of Chapter 3 is a revelation that shakes Alexander to his core. He discovers a hidden truth about his past that challenges his perception of freedom. This revelation forces him to re-evaluate his journey and the choices he has made. It is a moment of profound growth, as Alexander realizes that his quest for freedom is not just about breaking free from external constraints but also about confronting his inner demons.

Through Alexander's journey, i provides a nuanced examination of what it means to be truly free. The significance of Alexander's perspective on freedom and control is evident in the way it shapes his character and drives the narrative forward. The chapter leaves readers with a profound understanding of the delicate balance between freedom and control, and the importance of self-discipline in achieving true liberation.

The narrative voice, character interactions, and symbolic elements all contribute to a rich and thought-provoking exploration of these themes. Alexander's evolution from a naive seeker of physical liberty to a mature individual who understands the deeper implications of freedom and control is both compelling and enlightening. The chapter stands out as a pivotal moment in the story, setting the stage for further development and deeper introspection in the subsequent chapters.

Use of symbolism in Chief's hallucinations

Through these hallucinations, i delves into Chief's psyche, revealing his inner conflicts and the impact of his past experiences on his present state of mind. This analysis will dissect the symbolism embedded in Chief's hallucinations, examining how they contribute to character development and the narrative's thematic depth.

Chief's Hallucinations: A Gateway to the Subconscious.

Chief's hallucinations are not mere random occurrences but are deeply rooted in his subconscious mind. They act as a narrative device to peel back the layers of his character, revealing his fears, desires, and unresolved traumas. The hallucinations often manifest as surreal and fragmented scenes, reflecting the chaotic state of Chief's mind and his struggle to distinguish reality from illusion.

One recurring symbol in Chief's hallucinations is the image of the labyrinth. This labyrinth represents the complexities and confusion within Chief's mind. It symbolizes his internal struggle to navigate through his past traumas and the maze-like nature of his thoughts. The labyrinth is a metaphor for the intricate and often convoluted journey of self-discovery that Chief undergoes throughout the novel. Each turn and dead end in the labyrinth mirrors the challenges and setbacks Chief faces in his quest for clarity and understanding.

The Clock Tower: Time and Mortality.

Another prominent symbol in Chief's hallucinations is the clock tower. This symbol is laden with connotations of time, mortality, and the inexorable passage of life. The clock tower often appears in moments of acute anxiety or distress for Chief, underscoring his preoccupation with time and the fear of running out of it. The relentless ticking of the clock tower serves as a constant reminder of the fleeting nature of time and the inevitability of death, heightening Chief's sense of urgency and existential dread.

The clock tower also symbolizes the weight of Chief's past. It stands as a monolithic reminder of the events that have shaped him and the memories he cannot escape. The tower's imposing presence in his hallucinations suggests that Chief's past is ever-present, casting a long shadow over his current life. This symbolism is crucial in understanding Chief's character development, as it highlights the burden of his history and the difficulty of moving forward while being tethered to painful memories.

The Shattered Mirror: Identity and Fragmentation.

A particularly evocative symbol in Chief's hallucinations is the shattered mirror. This symbol represents the fragmentation of Chief's identity and his struggle to piece together a coherent sense of self. The broken mirror reflects Chief's fractured psyche, illustrating how his identity has been shattered by trauma and the conflicting narratives of his life. Each shard of the mirror holds a different facet of his personality or a different memory, suggesting a multiplicity of selves that Chief must reconcile.

The shattered mirror also symbolizes the distorted nature of Chief's self-perception. Just as a broken mirror distorts the reflection it casts, Chief's understanding of himself is warped by his hallucinations and the unreliable nature of his memories. This symbolism underscores the theme of unreliable narration, as the reader is left to question the authenticity of Chief's experiences and the extent to which his perceptions are shaped by his mental state.

The Raven: Omens and the Supernatural.

The raven is a recurring symbol in Chief's hallucinations, often appearing as a harbinger of doom or a messenger from the supernatural realm. In many cultures, the raven is associated with mystery, death, and the unknown, making it a fitting symbol for the dark and foreboding elements of Chief's subconscious. The raven's presence in Chief's hallucinations often coincides with moments of heightened tension or impending danger, serving as a symbolic warning of the challenges that lie ahead.

The raven also represents Chief's fear of the unknown and his sense of being haunted by unseen forces. This symbolism ties into the broader theme of paranoia and the feeling of being watched or pursued that permeates Chief's experiences. The raven's ominous presence highlights Chief's vulnerability and his constant state of unease, reinforcing the novel's exploration of the psychological impacts of trauma and the struggle to find safety and stability in a threatening world.

The River: Flow and Change.

The river is another significant symbol in Chief's hallucinations, representing the flow of life and the inevitability of change. The river's constant movement and the way it carves its path through the landscape symbolize the passage of time and the transformative journey that Chief is on. The river's waters are often depicted as murky and turbulent, reflecting the turmoil and uncertainty that characterize Chief's life.

The river also serves as a metaphor for the subconscious mind, with its hidden depths and currents. Just as the river's true nature is often obscured by its surface, Chief's true self is hidden beneath layers of hallucinations and distorted perceptions. The river's symbolism underscores the theme of exploration and the quest for self-discovery, as Chief must navigate the murky waters of his mind to uncover the truths that lie beneath.

The Forest: Wilderness and Isolation.

In Chief's hallucinations, the forest often appears as a symbol of wilderness and isolation. The dense, tangled undergrowth and the towering trees create a sense of enclosure and entrapment, reflecting Chief's feelings of being lost and alone. The forest represents the untamed and unpredictable aspects of Chief's psyche, where danger and uncertainty lurk around every corner.

The forest also symbolizes the primal and instinctual parts of Chief's nature. It is a place where he must confront his fears and the darker aspects of his personality. The isolation of the forest emphasizes Chief's sense of alienation and his struggle to connect with others. This symbolism highlights the novel's exploration of loneliness and the human need for connection, as Chief grapples with his feelings of being cut off from the world and from himself.

The Lighthouse: Guidance and Hope.

Amidst the dark and foreboding symbols in Chief's hallucinations, the lighthouse stands out as a beacon of hope and guidance. The lighthouse represents the possibility of finding direction and clarity in the midst of chaos. Its light cuts through the darkness, offering a path forward for Chief as he navigates the treacherous terrain of his mind.

The lighthouse also symbolizes the search for truth and understanding. Just as a lighthouse guides ships safely to shore, Chief's quest for truth and self-awareness is a journey towards enlightenment and resolution. The lighthouse's presence in his hallucinations suggests that despite the darkness and confusion, there is always a possibility of finding a guiding light and achieving a sense of clarity and purpose.

Chief's Hallucinations and Character Development.

Chief's hallucinations play a crucial role in his character development, serving as a window into his inner world and the forces that shape his identity. Through these hallucinations, i explores Chief's vulnerabilities, fears, and desires, providing a deeper understanding of his character and the motivations behind his actions.

The use of symbolism in Chief's hallucinations allows for a rich and nuanced portrayal of his psychological state. Each symbol carries multiple layers of meaning, reflecting the complexity of Chief's character and the intricate web of his experiences. The hallucinations serve as a narrative device to reveal the depth of Chief's struggles and the resilience he must summon to confront his demons.

Thematic Depth and Narrative Complexity.

The symbolism in Chief's hallucinations contributes significantly to the novel's thematic depth and narrative complexity. By weaving these symbols into the fabric of the story, i creates a multi-layered narrative that invites readers to delve deeper into the text and uncover the hidden meanings beneath the surface. The hallucinations serve as a metaphorical landscape where the novel's central themes of identity, trauma, and reality versus illusion are explored in a profound and thought-provoking manner.

The interplay between Chief's hallucinations and the narrative's broader themes adds a layer of complexity to the story, challenging readers to engage with the text on a deeper level. The use of symbolism encourages readers to question the nature of reality and the reliability of the narrator, adding to the novel's psychological and philosophical dimensions.

Through the use of symbols such as the labyrinth, the clock tower, the shattered mirror, the raven, the river, the forest, and the lighthouse, i delves into the depths of Chief's subconscious, revealing the complexities of his character and the thematic richness of the story. These symbols serve as a bridge between Chief's inner world and the external reality, offering insights into his struggles and the journey of self-discovery that defines his narrative arc.

Chapter 4: Randle McMurphy's Arrival

Introduction of McMurphy as a catalyst for change

In Ken Kesey's novel "One Flew Over the Cuckoo's Nest," the arrival of Randle P. McMurphy in Chapter 4 serves as a pivotal turning point in the narrative. His introduction marks the beginning of significant changes within the mental institution, affecting both the patients and the staff. This analysis will delve into how McMurphy's character functions as a catalyst for change, his impact on the other characters, and the broader implications of his presence in the ward.

McMurphy's Entrance and Initial Impact.

McMurphy's arrival is immediately notable due to his boisterous and confident demeanor, which starkly contrasts with the subdued and compliant nature of the other patients. His loud voice, bold mannerisms, and the way he carries himself all signal that he is different from the others. This stark difference is highlighted when he introduces himself with a firm handshake and a wide grin, exuding a sense of self-assurance that is foreign to the institutionalized environment.

The initial impact of McMurphy's presence is felt almost immediately. The patients, who have become accustomed to the oppressive and rigid routine of the ward, are taken aback by his audacity. His refusal to conform to the expected behavior of the institution disrupts the established order and introduces an element of unpredictability. This disruption is crucial as it begins to awaken the other patients from their passive acceptance of their circumstances.

Character Contrast and Conflict.

McMurphy's character is designed to be a foil to the antagonist, Nurse Ratched. While Nurse Ratched represents control, conformity, and the dehumanizing aspects of the institution, McMurphy embodies freedom, individuality, and rebellion. This contrast is evident from their very first interaction, where McMurphy's casual and irreverent attitude clashes with Nurse Ratched's cold and calculated demeanor.

The conflict between McMurphy and Nurse Ratched is not just a personal rivalry but a symbolic battle between individualism and institutionalization. McMurphy's defiance of the rules and his encouragement of the other patients to assert their own identities challenge the totalitarian control that Nurse Ratched exerts over the ward. This conflict becomes a central theme of the novel, driving the narrative forward and setting the stage for the climactic events.

Influence on Other Patients.

One of the most significant aspects of McMurphy's character is his influence on the other patients. His arrival sparks a sense of hope and rebellion among them. For instance, Chief Bromden, the novel's narrator, begins to see McMurphy as a potential savior who can liberate them from the oppressive environment. This is evident when Bromden describes McMurphy's laughter, which is something he hasn't heard in years, symbolizing a return to humanity and normalcy.

McMurphy's influence extends beyond Bromden to other patients like Harding and Billy Bibbit. Harding, who is initially skeptical and aloof, starts to admire McMurphy's courage and begins to question his own submission to the institution. Billy Bibbit, a timid and stuttering young man, finds a sense of empowerment through McMurphy's encouragement and begins to assert himself more.

The group therapy sessions, which were previously dominated by Nurse Ratched's manipulative tactics, start to change as McMurphy encourages the patients to speak up and challenge the nurse's authority. This shift in dynamics is significant as it represents the beginning of a collective awakening among the patients, who start to see the possibility of resistance and change.

Symbolism and Themes.

McMurphy's character is rich with symbolic meaning. He represents the spirit of rebellion and the fight against oppressive systems. His actions and demeanor challenge the dehumanizing effects of institutionalization, highlighting the importance of individuality and personal freedom. The fishing trip he organizes, for example, is a powerful symbol of liberation and self-discovery for the patients. It allows them to experience a sense of normalcy and camaraderie outside the confines of the ward.

The theme of power and control is also central to McMurphy's character. His struggle against Nurse Ratched's authority is a microcosm of the larger struggle against oppressive systems in society. Through McMurphy's defiance, Kesey critiques the ways in which institutions can dehumanize individuals and suppress their autonomy.

Transformation of the Ward.

The arrival of McMurphy brings about a transformation in the ward that is both subtle and profound. The patients, who were once passive and resigned to their fate, begin to exhibit signs of life and resistance. This transformation is not just psychological but also physical, as seen in their improved demeanor and increased participation in ward activities.

The change in the ward's atmosphere is also reflected in the way the patients interact with each other. There is a newfound sense of solidarity and camaraderie, as they start to see themselves as a community rather than isolated individuals. This sense of unity is crucial in their collective resistance against the oppressive regime of the institution.

Nurse Ratched's Response.

Nurse Ratched's response to McMurphy's arrival is telling of the threat he poses to her authority. Initially, she tries to dismiss him as a mere nuisance, but as his influence grows, she becomes increasingly threatened. Her tactics shift from passive-aggressive manipulation to more direct and aggressive measures to maintain control.

The escalating tension between McMurphy and Nurse Ratched culminates in a series of confrontations that highlight the power struggle within the ward. Nurse Ratched's attempts to break McMurphy's spirit and undermine his influence only serve to strengthen his resolve and solidify his role as a leader among the patients.

McMurphy in Chapter 4 of "One Flew Over the Cuckoo's Nest" is a turning point that sets the stage for the novel's exploration of themes such as individuality, freedom, and resistance against oppressive systems. McMurphy's character serves as a catalyst for change, disrupting the oppressive environment of the ward and inspiring the other patients to reclaim their sense of self. Through his defiance and influence, McMurphy challenges the dehumanizing effects of institutionalization and highlights the importance of personal freedom and autonomy. His arrival not only alters the dynamics of the ward but also drives the narrative forward, leading to the climactic events that define the novel's powerful message.

Examination of his rebellious spirit and charisma

McMurphy to the mental institution marks a pivotal moment that sets the stage for a profound exploration of rebellion and charisma. The chapter opens with McMurphy's introduction to the ward, characterized by his boisterous and unapologetic demeanor, which immediately sets him apart from the other patients. This section delves into McMurphy's character, highlighting his rebellious nature and magnetic personality, and examining how these traits impact the ward's dynamics and the other patients.

McMurphy's entrance is nothing short of theatrical. He strides into the ward with a swagger, wearing a leather jacket and a mischievous grin, immediately drawing attention to himself. This stark contrast to the subdued and compliant atmosphere of the ward is deliberate, signaling the arrival of a disruptive force. McMurphy's loud voice and confident stride are not just physical attributes but symbolic representations of his rebellious spirit. He refuses to conform to the institution's oppressive environment, choosing instead to assert his individuality loudly and proudly.

The Act of Rebellion: Challenging Authority.

One of the first indications of McMurphy's rebellious nature is his interaction with Nurse Ratched, the embodiment of the institution's oppressive authority. From their initial encounter, it is clear that McMurphy has no intention of submitting to her control. He questions her rules and authority, not out of ignorance but as a deliberate act of defiance. His refusal to be intimidated by her cold, calculating demeanor sets the tone for their ongoing battle of wills. This confrontation is crucial as it marks the beginning of McMurphy's role as a catalyst for change within the ward.

Charisma and Leadership: Rallying the Patients.

McMurphy's charisma is perhaps his most compelling trait. He possesses an innate ability to inspire and rally those around him. This is evident in how he quickly becomes the center of attention among the patients. His stories, jokes, and unfiltered commentary captivate the others, who are used to a life of monotony and repression. McMurphy's ability to make the patients laugh and feel a sense of camaraderie is a testament to his charismatic leadership.

His influence is further demonstrated when he organizes a betting pool on the World Series, an act that symbolizes his defiance of the institution's control over their lives. By encouraging the patients to participate in this seemingly trivial act of rebellion, McMurphy instills in them a sense of empowerment and solidarity. This small act of defiance becomes a symbol of their collective resistance against the oppressive regime of the ward.

The Impact on Other Characters.

McMurphy's arrival and subsequent actions have a profound impact on the other characters, particularly Chief Bromden, the novel's narrator. Chief Bromden, who has long been marginalized and perceived as deaf and dumb, begins to see McMurphy as a figure of hope and change. McMurphy's fearless demeanor and refusal to be subdued reignite a spark of defiance in Bromden, hinting at his potential for personal transformation.

Similarly, other patients such as Dale Harding and Billy Bibbit, who have been psychologically broken by the institution, start to show signs of awakening under McMurphy's influence. McMurphy's rebellious spirit challenges their perceptions of themselves and their environment, encouraging them to question the authority that has kept them subdued. This shift in their behavior underscores the transformative power of McMurphy's charisma and leadership.

Symbolism and Themes: The Rebellious Spirit as a Catalyst for Change.

McMurphy's character is laden with symbolism. He represents the indomitable human spirit that refuses to be crushed by oppressive systems. His rebellion is not just against the institution's rules but against the dehumanizing effects of conformity and control. Through McMurphy's actions, Kesey explores themes of individuality, freedom, and the human capacity for resistance.

The betting pool on the World Series, for instance, symbolizes more than just a wager; it represents the patients' reclaiming of their agency and the small victories that can be won through collective action. McMurphy's defiance becomes a beacon of hope, showing the other patients that resistance is possible and that they can reclaim their sense of self-worth and dignity.

The Battle of Wills: McMurphy vs. Nurse Ratched.

The ongoing battle between McMurphy and Nurse Ratched is a central conflict in the novel, highlighting the clash between individual freedom and institutional control. Nurse Ratched's authority is based on manipulation, intimidation, and the suppression of individuality. In contrast, McMurphy's rebellion is rooted in his inherent need for freedom and self-expression. This conflict is not just personal but ideological, reflecting broader societal tensions between conformity and rebellion.

McMurphy's tactics are often theatrical and provocative, designed to expose the absurdity and cruelty of the institution's rules. His actions force Nurse Ratched to reveal her true nature, stripping away the veneer of benevolence she maintains. This battle of wills becomes a microcosm of the larger struggle against oppressive systems, highlighting the importance of individual resistance in the face of authoritarian control.

McMurphy's Complexity: A Deeper Look.

While McMurphy is portrayed as a heroic figure, Kesey does not shy away from portraying his flaws and complexities. McMurphy's rebellious spirit is partly driven by his own need for self-preservation and a desire to assert his dominance. His charisma, while genuine, also serves his own interests. This complexity adds depth to his character, making him more than just a one-dimensional rebel.

McMurphy's past, including his criminal record and history of violence, hints at a darker side to his personality. His rebellion is not purely altruistic; it is also a means of asserting his own power and identity. This duality makes McMurphy a more nuanced and relatable character, reflecting the complexities of rebellion and leadership.

McMurphy's arrival injects a dose of rebellious energy into the ward, challenging the oppressive authority of Nurse Ratched and inspiring the other patients to reclaim their sense of self. His charismatic leadership and unapologetic defiance become catalysts for change, highlighting the transformative power of individual resistance. McMurphy's character, with all its flaws and complexities, embodies the indomitable human spirit, making him a timeless symbol of rebellion and hope. Through McMurphy, Kesey explores the profound impact of rebellion on both individuals and society, underscoring the importance of challenging oppressive systems and reclaiming personal freedom.

The initial clash with Nurse Ratched and the establishment

In Ken Kesey's novel "One Flew Over the Cuckoo's Nest," the arrival of Randle P. McMurphy in Chapter 4 serves as a pivotal moment that sets the stage for the ensuing conflict between the patients and the oppressive authority of Nurse Ratched. This chapter not only marks the introduction of a rebellious force into the ward but also lays the foundation for a deeper exploration of the characters' psyches and the oppressive system that governs their lives.

The Initial Clash with Nurse Ratched.

From the moment Randle P. McMurphy steps into the ward, his presence is a disruption to the meticulously controlled environment orchestrated by Nurse Ratched. His boisterous personality and defiant attitude starkly contrast with the subdued and compliant nature of the other patients. This clash is not merely a battle of wills between two individuals but a symbolic struggle between individualism and conformity, freedom and control.

Nurse Ratched, often referred to as "Big Nurse," is the embodiment of institutional authority and repression. Her cold, calculated demeanor and her meticulous control over the ward's routine reflect a broader commentary on the dehumanizing effects of institutionalization. She maintains her power through subtle manipulation and psychological control, ensuring that the patients remain docile and obedient.

McMurphy, on the other hand, is a force of chaotic energy and rebellion. His loud laughter, crude jokes, and open defiance of the ward's rules immediately challenge Nurse Ratched's authority. This initial clash is epitomized in their first interaction, where McMurphy's casual disregard for the rules and his attempt to assert his individuality are met with Nurse Ratched's cold, calculated response. Their confrontation is not just about breaking the rules; it's about challenging the very foundation of the institutionalized power structure.

Establishing the Conflict.

The establishment of this conflict in Chapter 4 is crucial to the narrative's development. McMurphy's arrival injects a sense of hope and defiance into the ward, awakening a spirit of resistance in the other patients. His presence disrupts the monotonous routine and exposes the underlying tensions within the ward. This disruption is essential for the narrative, as it forces the characters to confront their own fears and the oppressive reality of their situation.

McMurphy's behavior is not just a personal rebellion; it symbolizes a broader resistance against systemic oppression. His actions and attitude challenge the patients to question the status quo and consider the possibility of a different way of life. This is evident in the way he interacts with the other patients, encouraging them to stand up for themselves and to reclaim their sense of agency.

Character Development.

Randle P. McMurphy.

McMurphy's character is multifaceted and complex. He is portrayed as a larger-than-life figure, full of charisma and confidence. His background as a gambler and a brawler adds to his aura of toughness and resilience. However, beneath this tough exterior lies a deep sense of empathy and a desire to help his fellow patients. His motivations are not entirely selfless; he derives pleasure from defying authority and enjoys the chaos he creates. Yet, his actions are also driven by a genuine desire to empower the other patients and to challenge the oppressive system.

McMurphy's interactions with the other patients reveal different facets of his personality. He is a natural leader, able to inspire and rally the other patients. His relationship with Chief Bromden, the novel's narrator, is particularly significant. Through Chief Bromden's eyes, we see McMurphy as a heroic figure who brings a sense of purpose and hope to the ward. This relationship also allows for a deeper exploration of Chief Bromden's own character and his journey towards reclaiming his sense of self.

Nurse Ratched.

Nurse Ratched's character is equally complex and multi-dimensional. She is depicted as a cold, calculating figure who derives power from manipulating and controlling the patients. Her methods are subtle and insidious, relying on psychological manipulation rather than overt force. This approach makes her a formidable antagonist, as her control over the ward is almost absolute.

Her interactions with McMurphy reveal her vulnerabilities and the cracks in her seemingly impenetrable facade. McMurphy's defiance challenges her authority and exposes the limitations of her control. This dynamic creates a tension that drives the narrative forward, as both characters become increasingly determined to assert their dominance.

Thematic Exploration.

The clash between McMurphy and Nurse Ratched in Chapter 4 serves as a microcosm for the broader themes of the novel. It explores the conflict between individual freedom and institutional control, highlighting the dehumanizing effects of the latter. The ward, with its rigid routines and oppressive atmosphere, represents a larger critique of societal institutions that prioritize conformity and control over individual expression and autonomy.

McMurphy's rebellion is not just a personal battle; it is a symbol of the broader struggle against oppressive systems. His actions inspire the other patients to question their own submission and to consider the possibility of resistance. This theme is further explored through the interactions between the characters and the gradual awakening of their sense of agency.

Narrative Structure.

The narrative structure of the novel is intricately tied to the development of this conflict. The story is told from Chief Bromden's perspective, providing a unique insight into the dynamics of the ward and the impact of McMurphy's arrival. Chief Bromden's narrative is interspersed with his own internal struggles and hallucinations, adding a layer of complexity to the story.

The use of Chief Bromden as the narrator allows for a deeper exploration of the themes and characters. His perspective offers a nuanced view of McMurphy's rebellion and its impact on the other patients. It also allows for a more profound examination of the psychological effects of institutionalization and the struggle for individual identity.

Symbolism.

The clash between McMurphy and Nurse Ratched is rich with symbolism. McMurphy's red hair and boisterous personality symbolize passion, energy, and rebellion. In contrast, Nurse Ratched's cold, sterile appearance and demeanor represent control, repression, and dehumanization. The ward itself is a symbol of the larger society, with its rules and routines reflecting the broader societal norms and expectations.

This symbolism is further enhanced by the use of imagery and metaphors throughout the novel. The fog that frequently envelops Chief Bromden symbolizes his mental fog and the oppressive atmosphere of the ward. McMurphy's laughter, which is described as a force of nature, symbolizes his defiance and the awakening of the patients' spirits.

Impact on the Plot.

The initial clash between McMurphy and Nurse Ratched sets the stage for the rest of the novel. It establishes the central conflict and introduces the main themes and characters. This confrontation is not just a momentary dispute; it is the beginning of a prolonged battle that will have profound consequences for all the characters involved.

As the story progresses, this conflict intensifies, leading to a series of confrontations and escalating tensions. The impact of McMurphy's arrival is felt not only by the patients but also by Nurse Ratched, who becomes increasingly determined to maintain her control over the ward.

McMurphy and Nurse Ratched in Chapter 4 of "One Flew Over the Cuckoo's Nest" is a pivotal moment that sets the stage for the novel's exploration of themes such as freedom, control, and individual identity. This confrontation not only establishes the central conflict but also deepens the characterization of McMurphy and Nurse Ratched, revealing their complexities and the underlying tensions that drive the narrative. Through their interactions, Kesey offers a powerful critique of institutional oppression and the human spirit's capacity for resistance and resilience.

Chapter 5: The Struggle for Identity

Characters' struggles with their sense of self

Protagonist 1: Sarah.

Sarah's journey is emblematic of the broader theme of identity crisis. Throughout the novel, she is portrayed as a character in constant search of her true self, torn between the expectations of her family and her own desires.

Sarah's struggle is deeply rooted in her upbringing. Raised in a conservative household, she has always been expected to conform to traditional roles and values. Her family's rigid beliefs about gender roles and societal norms have left her feeling suffocated and disconnected from her true self. This dissonance is further exacerbated by her burgeoning awareness of her own ambitions and desires, which starkly contrast with the path laid out for her.

In this chapter, Sarah's internal turmoil is vividly depicted through her interactions with her family and her introspective moments. I employs a stream-of-consciousness narrative style to provide readers with a glimpse into Sarah's mind, revealing her fears, doubts, and aspirations. This narrative technique effectively conveys the depth of her struggle and the intense pressure she feels to either conform or rebel.

A pivotal scene in this chapter involves Sarah's confrontation with her mother, where she finally voices her dissatisfaction with the predetermined path. This confrontation is a turning point for Sarah, as it marks the first time she openly challenges her family's expectations. The emotional intensity of this scene underscores the significance of her struggle and sets the stage for her subsequent journey towards self-discovery.

Protagonist 2: David.

David's character arc in Chapter 5 is equally compelling, as he grapples with issues of identity and self-worth. Unlike Sarah, David's struggle is less about societal expectations and more about his own perception of himself. Haunted by a traumatic past and plagued by feelings of inadequacy, David's sense of self is fragile and fragmented.

Throughout the novel, David is depicted as a character who constantly seeks validation from others. His interactions are often driven by a desire to prove his worth, both to himself and to those around him. This need for external validation stems from a deep-seated insecurity that has been a part of him since childhood.

A significant event in this chapter is his reunion with an old friend, which forces him to confront painful memories and unresolved emotions. This confrontation acts as a catalyst for David's introspection, leading him to question the choices he has made and the person he has become.

I uses David's internal monologue to provide insight into his thought process and emotional state. Through David's reflections, readers gain a deeper understanding of the complexities of his character and the factors that have shaped his identity. This introspective approach highlights the theme of self-discovery and the arduous journey towards self-acceptance.

Supporting Characters: Their Influence on the Protagonists.

Supporting Character 1: Emily.

Emily plays a crucial role in Sarah's journey towards self-discovery. As Sarah's best friend, Emily serves as a foil to Sarah's character, embodying the freedom and confidence that Sarah longs for. Emily's unwavering support and encouragement provide Sarah with the strength to confront her fears and pursue her dreams.

She acts as a sounding board for Sarah's doubts and aspirations, offering a different perspective that challenges Sarah's preconceived notions about herself and her capabilities. Emily's character is instrumental in helping Sarah realize that her identity is not defined by others' expectations but by her own choices and actions.

Supporting Character 2: Michael.

Michael, David's mentor, plays a pivotal role in David's struggle for identity. As a father figure and confidant, Michael provides David with the guidance and support he desperately needs. Michael's wisdom and understanding help David navigate the complexities of his emotions and offer him a sense of stability in an otherwise tumultuous period of his life.

In this chapter, Michael's influence on David is evident in their heartfelt conversations. Michael's advice and encouragement encourage David to look beyond his insecurities and recognize his inherent worth. These interactions highlight the importance of mentorship and the impact it can have on one's self-perception and personal growth.

Thematic Exploration: Identity and Self-Discovery.

Chapter 5 of "The Struggle for Identity" delves deeply into the theme of identity and self-discovery. Through the protagonists' journeys, i explores the multifaceted nature of identity formation and the various factors that influence it. The characters' struggles with their sense of self are depicted with nuance and authenticity, making their experiences relatable and thought-provoking.

The theme of identity is intricately tied to the characters' interactions with their surroundings and the people in their lives. Sarah's conflict with her family and her desire to break free from societal norms reflect the broader struggle for individual autonomy and self-expression. Similarly, David's journey towards self-acceptance underscores the importance of introspection and the role of supportive relationships in shaping one's identity.

The author's use of rich, descriptive language and evocative imagery enhances the thematic exploration of identity. The settings and environments in which the characters find themselves are not merely backdrops but integral elements that contribute to their emotional and psychological states. The vivid descriptions of Sarah's hometown and David's childhood memories, for example, add depth to their narratives and provide context for their struggles.

Through the intricate character development and thematic exploration, i provides a profound insight into the complexities of identity formation and the inherent struggles that accompany this process. The nuanced portrayal of Sarah and David's experiences, along with the influence of supporting characters, offers a compelling narrative that resonates with readers on a deep emotional level. This chapter not only advances the plot but also enriches the overall thematic depth of the novel, making it a pivotal point in the characters' journeys towards understanding and accepting their true selves.

The impact of the institution on personal identity

The chapter delves into the lives of several key characters, examining how their interactions with various institutions—family, school, workplace, and society at large—impact their sense of self. This analysis will unpack the chapter's exploration of this theme through its plot and character development, providing a comprehensive understanding of the nuanced effects of institutional influence on personal identity.

Institutional Influence on Personal Identity.

1. Family as the Primary Institution.

The chapter begins by highlighting the family as the first and most fundamental institution that individuals encounter. For protagonist Alex, the family unit is depicted as both a source of comfort and a site of conflict. Alex's parents, traditional and conservative, impose their values and beliefs on him from a young age. This imposition creates a dichotomy within Alex; he struggles between adhering to his parents' expectations and exploring his own identity. The family's influence is portrayed as a double-edged sword—while providing a sense of belonging and security, it also imposes constraints that stifle Alex's personal growth. His eventual rebellion against these constraints marks the beginning of his journey towards self-discovery, illustrating the profound impact of familial expectations on personal identity.

2. Educational Institutions and Cognitive Molding.

The influence of educational institutions on identity is explored through the character of Sarah, a high-achieving student whose sense of worth is deeply intertwined with her academic success. The school system, with its emphasis on grades and performance, shapes Sarah's identity as a perfectionist. Her identity becomes contingent upon external validation, leading to an internalized pressure to excel. This dynamic is illustrated through Sarah's interactions with teachers and peers, where her self-esteem fluctuates based on academic feedback. The chapter poignantly depicts how the educational institution's focus on measurable achievement can overshadow the development of intrinsic self-worth, leading to a fragile and externally dependent identity.

3. Workplace and Professional Identity.

In the workplace, the characters of Mark and Lisa offer a look at how professional environments shape identity. Mark, an ambitious lawyer, finds his identity closely tied to his career success. The competitive nature of his law firm fosters a win-at-all-costs mentality, which initially propels Mark but eventually leads to ethical compromises and personal dissatisfaction. His identity crisis peaks when he realizes that his professional persona is at odds with his personal values. Similarly, Lisa's journey in a corporate setting reveals the pressure to conform to corporate culture, stifling her creativity and individuality. The chapter underscores how workplace institutions can enforce conformity, sometimes at the expense of personal authenticity.

4. Societal Institutions and Broader Identity Constructs.

The broader societal institutions—media, cultural norms, and social networks—also play a crucial role in shaping identity. Character David's storyline examines the impact of societal expectations on personal identity. Growing up in a culture that values traditional masculinity, David feels pressured to conform to these norms, suppressing his true self to fit in. The media's portrayal of idealized lifestyles and success further exacerbates his identity struggle, leading to a sense of inadequacy. This part of the chapter highlights the pervasive influence of societal institutions in constructing and reinforcing identity norms, often marginalizing those who do not fit the prescribed mold.

Character Development Through Institutional Interaction.

1. Alex: The Rebellious Self.

Alex's character arc is central to the chapter's exploration of institutional impact on identity. Initially compliant with his family's traditional values, Alex's journey is marked by a gradual awakening to his own desires and beliefs. The conflict between his family's expectations and his personal aspirations leads to significant internal turmoil. This tension culminates in a pivotal moment where Alex decides to pursue his passion for art, defying his parents' wish for him to become a doctor. This act of rebellion is not just against his family but against the institutionalized notion of success and identity imposed upon him. Alex's development illustrates the struggle for self-definition in the face of powerful institutional influences.

2. Sarah: The Perfectionist.

Sarah's character development provides a critical look at the impact of educational institutions on identity. Her journey through the education system is one of high achievement and equally high anxiety. The chapter details how Sarah's identity becomes increasingly defined by her academic achievements, to the detriment of her mental health. The pressure to maintain high grades and meet teachers' and parents' expectations leads to a perfectionist mindset. Sarah's eventual burnout and subsequent reevaluation of her self-worth highlight the damaging effects of an institutional focus on performance over personal well-being. Her story serves as a cautionary tale about the potential pitfalls of equating personal identity with external success.

3. Mark: The Ambitious Conformist.

Mark's narrative in the professional sphere offers a nuanced view of how workplace institutions shape identity. His initial alignment with the law firm's competitive culture brings him professional success but at a significant personal cost. The chapter portrays Mark's growing realization that his professional identity, built on ambition and conformity, conflicts with his personal values and ethics. This dissonance leads to a profound identity crisis, prompting Mark to reconsider his career choices and seek a path that aligns more closely with his true self. Mark's story illustrates the potential for institutions to both empower and constrain personal identity, highlighting the need for individuals to navigate these influences consciously.

4. Lisa: The Creative Nonconformist.

Lisa's character provides a counterpoint to Mark's experience in the workplace. Initially enthusiastic about her corporate job, Lisa soon finds herself stifled by the rigid corporate culture. Her creative approaches are often dismissed in favor of conventional methods, leading to a growing sense of frustration and alienation. Lisa's struggle against the institutional pressure to conform highlights the tension between personal creativity and institutional expectations. Her eventual decision to leave the corporate world and start her own business reflects a reclaiming of her identity, prioritizing personal fulfillment over institutional conformity. Lisa's journey underscores the importance of environments that nurture individual expression and the challenges posed by institutions that demand conformity.

5. David: The Search for Authenticity.

David's storyline offers a poignant exploration of the impact of societal institutions on personal identity. Growing up in a culture that enforces strict gender norms, David's journey is one of self-discovery and resistance. The chapter details his internal conflict as he grapples with societal expectations of masculinity, feeling pressured to conform while yearning to express his true self. The influence of media and cultural narratives further complicates his identity struggle, presenting idealized images of success and masculinity that David feels compelled to emulate. His eventual acceptance of his authentic self, despite societal pressures, marks a significant moment of personal liberation. David's story highlights the profound impact of societal institutions on identity and the courage required to defy these influences in pursuit of authenticity.

Chapter 5 of The Struggle for Identity provides a rich, multi-faceted exploration of how various institutions—family, education, workplace, and society—shape and influence personal identity. Through the detailed character arcs of Alex, Sarah, Mark, Lisa, and David, the chapter illustrates the complex interplay between institutional expectations and individual self-concept. Each character's journey reveals different facets of this theme, from the stifling effects of conformity to the liberating power of rebellion and self-acceptance.

The chapter ultimately suggests that while institutions play a significant role in shaping identity, individuals have the capacity to navigate and resist these influences in their quest for self-discovery. It underscores the importance of critical self-reflection and the courage to pursue personal authenticity in the face of institutional pressures. By examining the impact of institutional influence on personal identity, Chapter 5 offers valuable insights into the ongoing struggle for identity in a world governed by powerful social structures.

McMurphy's influence on the patients' sense of agency

Chapter 5 of "One Flew Over the Cuckoo's Nest" by Ken Kesey, titled "The Struggle for Identity," is a pivotal segment that delves into the transformative influence of Randall P. McMurphy on the patients at the mental institution. This chapter is particularly significant as it highlights the emergence of newfound agency among the patients, catalyzed by McMurphy's rebellious and charismatic presence.

At the beginning of the chapter, the patients' sense of self is largely suppressed by the oppressive machinery of the mental institution, symbolized by Nurse Ratched's authoritarian control. The men are depicted as docile, compliant, and stripped of their individuality. They are subjected to a rigid routine that stifles any semblance of personal autonomy. Nurse Ratched's manipulation tactics, including the use of shame, medication, and group therapy sessions that resemble inquisitions, further erode the patients' self-esteem and sense of agency.

McMurphy's arrival disrupts this oppressive equilibrium. His loud, boisterous demeanor and refusal to conform to the institution's rules immediately set him apart. From the moment he enters the ward, McMurphy challenges the status quo. He questions the arbitrary rules, mocks the institution's authority figures, and openly defies Nurse Ratched. This behavior is both shocking and inspiring to the other patients, who have long been conditioned to accept their powerlessness.

One of McMurphy's most significant acts in this chapter is his attempt to change the rigid schedule of the institution. He suggests a change in the television viewing time, a seemingly small request that is met with fierce resistance from Nurse Ratched. This request, though minor, symbolizes a larger struggle for autonomy and the right to make personal choices. The patients, who have been passive recipients of the institution's dictates, begin to see the possibility of challenging the system.

McMurphy's influence is further exemplified through his interactions with the other patients. He treats them with respect and camaraderie, which contrasts sharply with Nurse Ratched's condescending and dehumanizing approach. McMurphy's genuine interest in their lives and his encouragement of their individuality begin to revive their sense of self-worth. For instance, he engages Chief Bromden in conversations, acknowledging his presence and treating him as an equal. This simple act of recognition has a profound impact on Chief Bromden, who begins to emerge from his self-imposed silence and reclaim his identity.

The fishing trip organized by McMurphy in this chapter is another critical event that underscores his influence on the patients' sense of agency. The trip represents a break from the institution's control and an opportunity for the patients to experience a sense of freedom and normalcy. It is during this trip that the patients begin to assert themselves in small but meaningful ways. They make decisions, take risks, and support each other, behaviors that were previously suppressed by the institution's oppressive environment.

The transformation of the patients is also evident in their growing defiance towards Nurse Ratched. Inspired by McMurphy's example, they start to resist her authority in various ways. They become more vocal about their needs and desires, and they begin to question the legitimacy of her rules. This collective awakening is a direct result of McMurphy's influence, as he provides them with a model of resistance and self-assertion.

The climax of McMurphy's impact on the patients' sense of agency comes during a pivotal group therapy session. In this session, Nurse Ratched attempts to use her usual tactics of humiliation and manipulation to regain control. However, McMurphy's presence and the solidarity he has fostered among the patients disrupt her efforts. The patients, emboldened by

McMurphy's example, refuse to be cowed. They stand up to Nurse Ratched, challenging her authority and asserting their right to be heard.

McMurphy's influence extends beyond mere rebellion; he instills in the patients a sense of hope and possibility. He shows them that they are not defined by their diagnoses or by the institution's labels. Through his actions and his unwavering belief in their inherent worth, he helps them rediscover their identities and their capacity for self-determination.

This chapter also highlights the risks and costs associated with asserting agency in an oppressive system. McMurphy's defiance does not go unanswered. Nurse Ratched retaliates with increased aggression, using her authority to punish the patients and reassert her control. This escalation underscores the dangerous power dynamics at play and the high stakes involved in challenging an entrenched system.

Through his defiance, camaraderie, and unwavering belief in their inherent worth, McMurphy reawakens the patients' sense of self and their capacity for resistance. This chapter is a testament to the transformative power of solidarity and the enduring human spirit in the face of oppression. McMurphy's legacy is one of empowerment, as he leaves an indelible mark on the patients, inspiring them to reclaim their identities and assert their right to self-determination.

Chapter 6: The Role of Femininity and Masculinity

Analysis of Nurse Ratched's embodiment of patriarchal control

Nurse Ratched, also known as Mildred Ratched, is one of the most iconic characters in Ken Kesey's novel "One Flew Over the Cuckoo's Nest." Her character serves as a powerful symbol of patriarchal control within the confines of a mental institution, where she wields her authority with an iron fist.

Nurse Ratched's Embodiment of Patriarchal Control.

Authority and Domination.

Nurse Ratched's character is the epitome of authoritarian control. She rules the ward with an unyielding hand, using her position to enforce strict discipline and order. Her control is not merely a result of her professional role but is deeply rooted in her ability to manipulate and intimidate the patients. She maintains her power by instilling fear and dependency among the men, ensuring that they see her as the ultimate authority figure.

Nurse Ratched's dominance is particularly evident in her interactions with the patients. She uses her power to humiliate and emasculate them, often through subtle psychological tactics rather than overt aggression. For example, she exposes the patients' vulnerabilities by reading their medical records aloud, exploiting their insecurities and undermining their sense of self. This tactic not only reinforces her control but also serves to remind the patients of their supposed inferiority.

Suppression of Masculinity.

One of the most striking aspects of Nurse Ratched's character is her systematic suppression of masculinity. The ward is a microcosm of society, reflecting broader societal norms and gender roles. Nurse Ratched's efforts to control and suppress the men's masculinity can be seen as a reflection of the broader societal pressures to conform to traditional gender roles.

She often uses her authority to emasculate the patients, stripping them of their dignity and autonomy. This is evident in her treatment of characters like Randle P. McMurphy, whose rebellious and overtly masculine behavior poses a direct threat to her authority. Nurse Ratched's efforts to control McMurphy are not just about maintaining order; they are about maintaining her dominance over the male patients. She uses various methods, including medication, electroconvulsive therapy, and manipulation of the patients' social dynamics, to keep them subdued.

Use of Surveillance and Manipulation.

Surveillance and manipulation are key tools in Nurse Ratched's arsenal of control. She employs a network of informants among the patients, such as the character of Charles Cheswick, who feed her information about the other patients' activities and conversations. This constant surveillance ensures that any potential rebellion is swiftly quashed, and it reinforces the patients' sense of being constantly watched and judged.

Nurse Ratched's manipulation is also evident in her control over the environment of the ward. She carefully orchestrates the daily routines and activities to maintain a sense of order and predictability, which serves to further entrench her authority. The rigid structure of the ward, with its strict schedules and lack of personal freedom, reflects the oppressive nature of patriarchal control.

Psychological Warfare.

Nurse Ratched's use of psychological warfare is perhaps her most insidious method of control. She understands the psychological vulnerabilities of her patients and exploits them to maintain her power. Her ability to manipulate the patients' emotions and perceptions is a testament to her deep understanding of human psychology.

For instance, she uses group therapy sessions not as a means of healing but as a tool for control. These sessions often devolve into opportunities for the patients to attack and undermine each other, with Nurse Ratched subtly guiding the conversations to sow discord and maintain her dominance. By creating an environment of suspicion and competition, she ensures that the patients remain divided and easier to control.

Character Development and Symbolism.

Nurse Ratched as a Symbol of Patriarchal Oppression.

Nurse Ratched's character can be seen as a symbol of patriarchal oppression. Her authoritarian rule over the ward mirrors the broader societal structures that oppress and control individuals. In a literary sense, she represents the oppressive forces that seek to maintain the status quo and suppress any form of rebellion or dissent.

Her character also highlights the intersection of gender and power dynamics. As a woman in a position of authority, she subverts traditional gender roles, yet she uses her power to reinforce the very patriarchal structures that typically oppress women. This complex portrayal adds depth to her character and underscores the nuanced ways in which power and control operate within society.

The Impact on Male Characters.

The impact of Nurse Ratched's control on the male characters is profound. Characters like Chief Bromden and Billy Bibbit are deeply affected by her authoritarian rule. Chief Bromden, the novel's narrator, is particularly significant in this regard. His perception of Nurse Ratched as a powerful and oppressive figure reflects his broader feelings of powerlessness and disenfranchisement.

Billy Bibbit's tragic fate is a direct result of Nurse Ratched's manipulation. Her emasculating tactics and psychological abuse lead to his ultimate breakdown and suicide. This highlights the destructive consequences of patriarchal control and the devastating effects it can have on individuals' mental health and sense of self-worth.

Nurse Ratched's embodiment of patriarchal control in "One Flew Over the Cuckoo's Nest" serves as a powerful critique of authoritarianism and the oppressive nature of societal norms. Through her character, Ken Kesey explores the ways in which power, control, and manipulation are used to maintain dominance over others. Nurse Ratched's authoritarian rule, suppression of masculinity, use of surveillance and manipulation, and psychological warfare all contribute to her role as a symbol of patriarchal oppression.

Her character's impact on the male patients underscores the destructive consequences of such control, highlighting the importance of resistance and the fight for autonomy and dignity. In analyzing Nurse Ratched's character, we gain a deeper understanding of the complex dynamics of power and gender in society, and the ways in which they shape individuals' lives and experiences.

McMurphy's challenge to traditional gender roles

In Ken Kesey's novel "One Flew Over the Cuckoo's Nest," the character of Randle P. McMurphy emerges as a potent and subversive force against the established norms of femininity and masculinity within the confines of the psychiatric ward. Chapter 6, in particular, provides a critical lens through which to examine how McMurphy's presence and actions challenge traditional gender roles, reshaping the dynamics of power and identity within the institution.

McMurphy's challenge to traditional gender roles is evident from his very introduction into the ward. The psychiatric ward is depicted as a microcosm of society, governed by Nurse Ratched, who represents the rigid, emasculating, and controlling aspects of femininity. She maintains order through manipulation, surveillance, and psychological intimidation, embodying the archetype of the castrating female authority figure. Nurse Ratched's control is not merely administrative; it extends into the emotional and psychological realms, where she seeks to dominate and emasculate the male patients, stripping them of their autonomy and masculinity.

McMurphy, on the other hand, represents a raw, unapologetic form of masculinity. His arrival disrupts the ward's carefully maintained balance of power. He is loud, rebellious, and overtly sexual, traits that starkly contrast with the sterile, controlled environment fostered by Nurse Ratched. From the moment he steps into the ward, McMurphy begins to challenge Nurse Ratched's authority and, by extension, the traditional gender roles she enforces.

One of the first and most significant challenges to traditional gender roles comes through McMurphy's interactions with the other patients. He quickly identifies the emasculating effect Nurse Ratched has on them and sets out to restore their sense of masculinity. This is seen when McMurphy organizes a fishing trip, an activity that is traditionally male-dominated and associated with masculinity. The trip serves as a form of rebellion against Nurse Ratched's control and a means for the patients to reclaim their sense of self-worth and manhood. It is a direct affront to the emasculating environment Nurse Ratched has created, where male patients are infantilized and stripped of their agency.

McMurphy's challenge to traditional gender roles is also evident in his sexuality. He is unapologetically sexual, using his charisma and virility as tools of resistance against Nurse Ratched's sterile, asexual regime. His sexual confidence and openness about his sexual experiences stand in direct opposition to the repressed and controlled sexual expression Nurse Ratched enforces. This is particularly evident in his interactions with the female staff and patients, where he flaunts his sexuality as a means of asserting his dominance and challenging the power structure.

Moreover, McMurphy's relationship with Nurse Ratched can be seen as a battleground for traditional gender roles. Their interactions are laden with sexual tension and power struggles, reflecting broader societal conflicts over gender and power. Nurse Ratched's attempts to control and emasculate McMurphy are met with his relentless defiance and sexual bravado. This dynamic is most poignantly illustrated in the scene where McMurphy exposes himself to Nurse Ratched, a shocking and defiant act that undermines her authority and highlights the absurdity of her attempts to control and suppress male sexuality.

The fishing trip organized by McMurphy serves as a critical turning point in the narrative. It is during this trip that the patients begin to break free from Nurse Ratched's control and rediscover their masculinity. The trip is not just a physical escape from the ward but a symbolic reclaiming of their identities as men. McMurphy's leadership and encouragement allow the patients to experience a sense of freedom and self-worth that has been long denied to them. The fishing trip becomes a metaphor for the broader struggle against oppressive gender norms and the reclaiming of one's identity in the face of societal constraints.

McMurphy's influence extends beyond the male patients to Nurse Ratched herself. Her authority begins to crumble as McMurphy's presence and actions expose the cracks in her carefully constructed façade. The more McMurphy challenges her control, the more she is forced to confront her own vulnerabilities and the limitations of her power. This is evident in her increasingly desperate attempts to reassert her authority, which ultimately lead to her psychological breakdown.

Through his rebellious actions, unapologetic sexuality, and leadership, McMurphy subverts the oppressive gender dynamics enforced by Nurse Ratched. His presence in the ward serves as a catalyst for the patients' journey towards reclaiming their masculinity and their sense of self. McMurphy's character embodies the struggle against oppressive gender norms, offering a powerful critique of the ways in which traditional gender roles can be used to control and suppress individuals. His defiance and resilience ultimately expose the fragility of Nurse Ratched's authority and the arbitrary nature of the gender roles she seeks to enforce.

The interplay of power dynamics between characters

The Role of Femininity.

Femininity in the narrative is multifaceted, encompassing both traditional and subversive elements. Female characters navigate a landscape where their power is often derived from, or in opposition to, their perceived femininity.

Traditional Femininity.

Traditional femininity is represented by characters who adhere to societal norms and expectations. These characters often wield power through manipulation, emotional intelligence, and social influence rather than overt authority.

Character 1: The Matriarch.

The Matriarch, a central female character, embodies traditional femininity. She is depicted as the backbone of her family, using her influence to guide and protect her kin. Her power is subtle, exercised through nurturing and wisdom rather than force. This approach to power is effective within the family structure, where emotional bonds are paramount.

Character 2: The Siren.

The Siren represents another facet of traditional femininity, using her allure and charm to manipulate those around her. Her power lies in her ability to captivate and control through seduction and emotional appeal. This character demonstrates how traditional feminine traits can be weaponized to achieve personal goals, often at the expense of others.

Subversive Femininity.

In contrast, subversive femininity challenges traditional norms, with characters using their femininity in unconventional ways to assert power.

Character 3: The Rebel.

The Rebel is a character who defies traditional feminine roles, seeking power through independence and rebellion. Her strength comes from rejecting societal expectations and forging her own path. This character's journey highlights the conflict between individual identity and societal norms, showcasing the power of self-determination and authenticity.

Character 4: The Strategist.

The Strategist uses intellect and strategic thinking to navigate a male-dominated world. Her femininity is not a weakness but a tool she leverages to gain an advantage. This character exemplifies how intelligence and cunning can subvert traditional power structures, offering a counter-narrative to the idea that femininity is inherently passive or subordinate.

The Role of Masculinity.

Masculinity in the narrative is equally complex, with characters embodying both traditional and progressive forms of male power.

Traditional Masculinity.

Traditional masculinity is often associated with strength, dominance, and control. Male characters who embody these traits typically hold positions of authority and exert their power directly.

Character 5: The Patriarch.

The Patriarch represents traditional masculinity, holding sway over his family and community through authority and physical strength. His power is overt, relying on dominance and control to maintain order. This character's approach to power often leads to conflict, especially when challenged by those who do not conform to traditional roles.

Character 6: The Warrior.

The Warrior embodies the physical aspects of masculinity, using strength and bravery to assert his power. His identity is closely tied to his ability to protect and defend, reflecting societal expectations of male heroism. However, this character's journey often reveals the limitations and costs of such a narrow view of masculinity.

Progressive Masculinity.

Progressive masculinity challenges traditional norms, with characters embracing vulnerability, empathy, and collaboration.

Character 7: The Caregiver.

The Caregiver represents a progressive view of masculinity, prioritizing empathy and care over dominance. His power is derived from his ability to nurture and support, challenging the notion that strength is solely physical. This character's approach to power fosters cooperation and mutual respect, offering a more inclusive model of masculinity.

Character 8: The Diplomat.

The Diplomat uses communication and understanding to navigate conflicts, embodying a collaborative approach to power. His masculinity is expressed through diplomacy and negotiation rather than force, highlighting the strength found in empathy and compromise. This character demonstrates how progressive masculinity can lead to more sustainable and harmonious power dynamics.

Interplay of Power Dynamics.

The interplay of power dynamics between characters is a central theme in Chapter 6, illustrating how femininity and masculinity influence relationships and plot development.

Conflict and Cooperation.

Conflicts often arise from clashes between traditional and progressive views of femininity and masculinity. For example, the Matriarch's subtle influence may clash with the Patriarch's authoritarian approach, creating tension within the family. Similarly, the Rebel's defiance of traditional roles can lead to conflict with characters who adhere to conventional norms.

Cooperation, on the other hand, is often found when characters recognize and respect each other's strengths, regardless of gender. The Strategist and the Diplomat, for instance, may find common ground through their shared emphasis on intelligence and empathy, working together to achieve common goals.

Character Development.

The development of characters is deeply influenced by their engagement with power dynamics. Characters who challenge traditional roles often experience significant growth, learning to balance their identities with societal expectations. The Rebel, for instance, may find a way to assert her independence while still honoring her familial responsibilities.

Conversely, characters who adhere strictly to traditional roles may face challenges that force them to reconsider their views. The Patriarch, for example, might encounter situations that require empathy and cooperation, leading to personal growth and a more nuanced understanding of power.

Through the nuanced portrayal of characters like the Matriarch, the Rebel, the Patriarch, and the Diplomat, the narrative highlights the complexities of power and the potential for growth and change. By understanding these dynamics, readers gain insight into the broader themes of identity, society, and the multifaceted nature of power itself.

Chapter 7: Rebellion and Its Consequences

Exploration of the various forms of rebellion within the institution

The Protagonist's Rebellion.

The protagonist, who has thus far navigated the institution with a sense of cautious compliance, begins to exhibit a more overt form of rebellion in this chapter. Their journey from subtle defiance to outright resistance is marked by several key events that illustrate their growing discontent and determination to challenge the status quo.

1. Intellectual Rebellion: The protagonist starts by questioning the institution's rules and norms. This form of rebellion is primarily internal and intellectual. They engage in critical thinking, analyzing the institution's justifications for its policies and identifying the inherent contradictions and hypocrisies. This mental rebellion is crucial as it lays the foundation for more tangible forms of resistance.

2. Moral Rebellion: As the protagonist becomes more aware of the institution's moral failings, they begin to take a stand based on their ethical beliefs. This is seen in their refusal to participate in activities that they deem unjust or immoral. For example, they might refuse to follow orders that involve mistreatment of fellow inmates or the perpetuation of falsehoods. This moral stance often puts them at odds with the institution's authorities and their collaborators.

3. Active Rebellion: The protagonist's rebellion becomes more active as they start to take concrete actions against the institution. This can involve

organizing or participating in acts of defiance, such as protests, strikes, or sabotage. These actions are risky and often met with severe consequences, but they are essential for the protagonist to assert their agency and challenge the institution's power.

The Antagonist's Counter-Rebellion.

In response to the protagonist's rebellion, the institution and its representatives also undergo a transformation. The antagonist, typically a figure of authority within the institution, adopts various strategies to quell the rebellion and maintain control.

1. Surveillance and Intimidation: The antagonist increases surveillance of the protagonist and their allies. This is done through both overt methods, such as increased security measures and monitoring, and covert methods, such as informants and spies. The goal is to gather intelligence on the rebellion and intimidate potential rebels into submission.

2. Propaganda and Manipulation: The antagonist uses propaganda to discredit the rebellion and its leaders. This can involve spreading misinformation, sowing discord among the rebels, and portraying the institution in a positive light. The aim is to undermine the legitimacy of the rebellion and ensure the loyalty of other inmates or members of the institution.

3. Punishment and Coercion: When surveillance and propaganda fail, the antagonist resorts to direct punishment and coercion. This can involve physical punishment, solitary confinement, or other forms of retribution. The antagonist may also use psychological coercion, such as threatening loved ones or promising leniency in exchange for compliance.

The Role of Supporting Characters.

Supporting characters play a crucial role in the unfolding drama of rebellion and its consequences. They provide various forms of support, resistance, and complicity that shape the narrative.

1. Allies: Allies are characters who join the protagonist in their rebellion. They share similar grievances and are motivated by a desire for change. These characters often come from diverse backgrounds, bringing different skills and perspectives to the rebellion. Their solidarity with the protagonist strengthens the resistance and provides a counterbalance to the institution's power.

2. Bystanders: Bystanders are characters who, while not actively participating in the rebellion, also do not actively oppose it. They may sympathize with the rebels but are too afraid or unwilling to take a stand. Their inaction can be seen as a form of tacit support for the institution, as it allows the status quo to persist.

3. Collaborators: Collaborators are characters who actively support the institution and oppose the rebellion. They may do so out of self-interest, fear, or genuine belief in the institution's values. Collaborators often serve as informants or enforcers for the antagonist, helping to maintain control and suppress dissent.

Consequences of Rebellion.

The consequences of rebellion are far-reaching and impact all characters involved. These consequences are explored in depth, highlighting the personal and collective costs of defiance.

1. Personal Consequences: The protagonist and their allies face significant personal risks. They may suffer physical harm, psychological trauma, or loss of freedom. The institution's punishments are designed to break their spirit and serve as a deterrent to others. Despite these risks, the characters' commitment to their cause often provides them with a sense of purpose and resilience.

2. Institutional Consequences: The rebellion also has consequences for the institution itself. It can expose weaknesses and contradictions within the institution, leading to internal conflicts and crises of legitimacy. The

institution may be forced to implement reforms or, conversely, may become more repressive in its efforts to maintain control.

3. Collective Consequences: The rebellion has broader implications for the community within and outside the institution. It can inspire others to resist, leading to a broader movement for change. Alternatively, it can result in increased repression and a clampdown on dissent. The outcome often depends on the balance of power and the ability of the rebels to sustain their resistance.

Analysis of Key Events.

Several key events in Chapter 7 serve to illustrate the themes of rebellion and its consequences.

1. The Spark: The chapter begins with an inciting incident that sparks the protagonist's active rebellion. This event, often a dramatic injustice or a moment of personal crisis, galvanizes the protagonist into taking a stand. It serves as a catalyst for the rebellion and sets the stage for subsequent events.

2. The Climax: The climax of the chapter involves a major confrontation between the rebels and the institution. This can be a physical confrontation, such as a protest or a riot, or a strategic maneuver, such as a mass escape or a plot to expose the institution's wrongdoing. The climax is the point of highest tension and drama, where the stakes are at their highest.

3. The Aftermath: The aftermath of the rebellion explores the immediate and long-term consequences for the characters and the institution. This can involve a reckoning with the costs of rebellion, an assessment of what has been achieved, and the beginning of new challenges or conflicts. The aftermath provides closure to the immediate narrative while setting up future developments.

Character Development.

The exploration of rebellion and its consequences is deeply intertwined with character development. The experiences of the protagonist and other characters reveal their true nature and motivations, as well as their capacity for growth and change.

1. Protagonist's Growth: The protagonist undergoes significant growth as a result of their rebellion. They become more self-aware, resilient, and committed to their values. This growth is often marked by moments of doubt and struggle, as they confront the full weight of the institution's power and the personal sacrifices required for their cause.

2. Antagonist's Complexity: The antagonist is also developed in complexity, revealing the motivations and pressures that drive their actions. This can involve a backstory that provides context for their role in the institution, as well as moments of internal conflict and doubt. The antagonist's complexity adds depth to the narrative, making them more than just a villain.

3. Supporting Characters' Roles: The supporting characters are developed through their interactions with the protagonist and their responses to the rebellion. Their individual stories and motivations are explored, providing a rich tapestry of perspectives on the rebellion and its impact.

Themes and Symbolism.

Chapter 7 employs various themes and symbols to deepen the exploration of rebellion and its consequences.

1. Themes of Freedom and Oppression: The central theme of the chapter is the struggle between freedom and oppression. The protagonist's rebellion is a quest for autonomy and justice, while the institution represents the forces of control and repression. This theme is explored through the characters' actions and the consequences they face.

2. Symbols of Rebellion: Various symbols are used to represent the rebellion and its significance. These can include objects, such as a forbidden book or a hidden weapon, as well as actions, such as a secret meeting or a daring escape. These symbols serve to underscore the themes of resistance and defiance.

3. Imagery of Confinement and Liberation: The chapter uses imagery of confinement and liberation to highlight the stakes of the rebellion. The institution is depicted as a place of imprisonment, both physical and psychological, while the rebellion is portrayed as a means of breaking free from these constraints. This imagery reinforces the narrative's core conflict.

Chapter 7 of the book provides a rich and nuanced exploration of rebellion within an oppressive institution. Through the experiences of the protagonist and other characters, the chapter examines the various forms of rebellion, the strategies used to suppress it, and the far-reaching consequences for all involved. The narrative delves into the personal and collective dimensions of rebellion, highlighting the themes of freedom, oppression, and the quest for justice. The character development and use of themes and symbols contribute to a compelling and thought-provoking exploration of rebellion and its consequences.

The ramifications of McMurphy's defiance

In Ken Kesey's seminal novel "One Flew Over the Cuckoo's Nest," Chapter 7 is a pivotal juncture where the consequences of Randle P. McMurphy's rebellion against the oppressive regime of Nurse Ratched begin to crystallize. This chapter serves as a microcosm of the broader themes of the novel, highlighting the conflict between individual autonomy and institutional control, the power dynamics within the ward, and the psychological warfare that ensues.

The Setting: The Chronics and Acutes.

The ward is divided into two main groups: the Chronics, who are physically or mentally incapacitated, and the Acutes, who are considered treatable. These groups serve as a backdrop to McMurphy's defiance and the ripple effects it creates within the institutional hierarchy. The Chronics symbolize the extreme result of institutional control, while the Acutes represent the potential for resistance and change.

McMurphy's Arrival and Initial Defiance.

From the moment McMurphy arrives, his presence is disruptive. He introduces a sense of normalcy and humor into the sterile environment of the ward, challenging the dehumanizing routine imposed by Nurse Ratched. His early acts of defiance—questioning the rules, making jokes, and asserting his individuality—set the stage for the larger rebellion in Chapter 7.

The Fishing Trip Proposal.

The fishing trip symbolizes freedom, normalcy, and the possibility of life beyond the institution's walls. McMurphy's insistence on this trip is not just about the activity itself but about reclaiming a sense of agency and self-worth for the patients.

The Group Meeting.

The group therapy session led by Nurse Ratched in Chapter 7 becomes a battleground for control. She uses the meeting to undermine McMurphy's influence, subtly manipulating the patients' perceptions of him. Her tactic is to paint McMurphy as a disruptive force whose actions could lead to negative consequences for the patients. This meeting highlights the psychological warfare at play, where Nurse Ratched's calm demeanor masks her insidious control over the patients' minds.

The Ramifications of Defiance.

McMurphy's defiance has several significant ramifications:

1. Solidarity Among Patients: McMurphy's actions foster a sense of solidarity among the Acutes. His willingness to stand up to Nurse Ratched inspires them to consider their own potential for resistance. This budding solidarity is crucial as it begins to erode the power dynamics that Nurse Ratched relies on to maintain control.

2. Increased Surveillance and Control: In response to McMurphy's rebellion, Nurse Ratched tightens her control over the ward. She implements stricter rules and increases surveillance, creating an atmosphere of tension and fear. This reaction underscores the institution's reliance on discipline and order to suppress individuality and dissent.

3. Psychological Impact on Patients: The psychological impact of McMurphy's defiance is profound. For some patients, it sparks a glimmer of hope and a desire for change. For others, it exacerbates their fear of retribution. This dichotomy reflects the broader human experience of balancing the desire for freedom with the fear of consequences.

4. Nurse Ratched's Frustration: Nurse Ratched's frustration with McMurphy's defiance becomes increasingly evident. Her composure begins to crack, revealing the extent to which her authority is threatened by his actions. Her struggle to maintain control highlights the fragility of institutional power when faced with determined resistance.

The Role of Bromden.

Chief Bromden, the novel's narrator, provides a unique perspective on McMurphy's rebellion. As a Chronic who has feigned deafness and muteness to escape the institution's demands, Bromden's observations offer insight into the deeper impact of McMurphy's actions. Bromden's growing awareness and eventual participation in the rebellion signify a personal transformation that mirrors the broader changes within the ward.

The Climactic Confrontation.

The climax of Chapter 7 is the confrontation between McMurphy and Nurse Ratched during the group meeting. This confrontation is a turning point in their power struggle. McMurphy's refusal to back down, despite the risks, underscores his commitment to challenging the institution's control. Nurse Ratched's response, marked by a calculated escalation of psychological pressure, reveals her willingness to use the patients' vulnerabilities against them.

The Broader Implications.

The events of Chapter 7 have broader implications for the novel's exploration of themes such as power, control, and individuality. McMurphy's rebellion is not merely an act of defiance but a catalyst for a larger movement towards personal and collective liberation. His actions force the patients to confront their own fears and limitations, prompting a reevaluation of their place within the institution.

Character Development.

His actions demonstrate his deep empathy and commitment to empowering others, even at great personal risk.

Nurse Ratched: Her character is further revealed as a master manipulator whose control is maintained through psychological manipulation and coercion. The chapter exposes the lengths to which she will go to maintain her authority.

The Patients: The patients' development is marked by a growing awareness of their own agency. McMurphy's influence prompts them to question the status quo and consider the possibility of a life beyond institutional control.

The Symbolism of the Fishing Trip.

The proposed fishing trip is rich with symbolic meaning. It represents a break from the oppressive environment of the ward and a return to a more natural, human state of being. The trip's symbolism extends to themes of freedom, self-discovery, and the healing power of nature. By proposing the trip, McMurphy is not only challenging Nurse Ratched's authority but also offering the patients a vision of a life worth living.

Chapter 7 of "One Flew Over the Cuckoo's Nest" is a critical exploration of the ramifications of defiance in the face of institutional control. McMurphy's actions serve as a catalyst for change, challenging the power dynamics within the ward and inspiring the patients to reclaim their sense of self. The chapter's events underscore the novel's broader themes and set the stage for the escalating conflict between individuality and institutional oppression. Through McMurphy's rebellion, Kesey highlights the enduring struggle for personal freedom and the profound impact of resistance in the face of systemic control.

Discussion of how rebellion leads to both liberation and repression

Chapter 7 of "Rebellion and Its Consequences" delves into the complex interplay between rebellion, liberation, and repression. The chapter meticulously explores how acts of rebellion, while often aimed at achieving freedom and justice, can paradoxically lead to new forms of repression and control. This dual nature of rebellion is a central theme that underscores the narrative, shaping the development of key characters and the unfolding of the plot. This analysis will provide a detailed examination of how rebellion manifests in the lives of the characters, the consequences they face, and the broader implications for the society depicted in the novel.

The Nature of Rebellion.

Rebellion in Chapter 7 is portrayed as a multifaceted phenomenon, encompassing both ideological and physical resistance. The characters' motivations for rebelling are varied, ranging from personal grievances to broader societal injustices. This diversity of motivations reflects the complex nature of rebellion itself, which is not monolithic but rather a spectrum of actions and ideologies.

1. Personal Rebellion:

Personal rebellion is exemplified by characters like Lena, who rebels against the strictures imposed by her family and society. Lena's defiance is rooted in her desire for self-determination and the pursuit of her own identity. Her journey highlights the liberating aspects of rebellion, as she breaks free from the constraints that have been placed upon her. However, this liberation comes at a cost, as Lena faces significant social and emotional repercussions for her actions. Her struggle underscores the tension between individual autonomy and societal expectations, illustrating how personal rebellion can lead to both empowerment and isolation.

2. Societal Rebellion:

On a broader scale, societal rebellion is depicted through the actions of characters like Marcus, who leads a revolutionary movement against an oppressive regime. Marcus's rebellion is driven by a vision of a more just and equitable society. His actions are portrayed as heroic and necessary, yet they also bring about significant upheaval and violence. The narrative explores the double-edged sword of societal rebellion, where the quest for liberation often involves destruction and loss. The consequences of Marcus's rebellion reveal how the pursuit of collective freedom can inadvertently lead to new forms of repression, as power vacuums and conflicts arise in the wake of the old order's collapse.

The Consequences of Rebellion.

The consequences of rebellion are a central focus of Chapter 7, highlighting the intricate balance between liberation and repression. The narrative demonstrates that rebellion, while necessary for progress and change, also carries inherent risks and potential negative outcomes.

1. Liberation:

The liberating effects of rebellion are evident in the newfound freedoms and opportunities that emerge for some characters. Lena, for instance, experiences a profound sense of liberation as she defies societal norms and asserts her independence. This liberation is not only personal but also symbolic, representing the broader struggle for individual rights and self-expression. Similarly, Marcus's revolutionary efforts lead to the overthrow of a tyrannical regime, resulting in greater political and social freedoms for the populace. These moments of liberation are depicted as triumphant and transformative, underscoring the potential of rebellion to bring about positive change.

2. Repression:

However, the narrative also delves into the darker side of rebellion, illustrating how it can lead to new forms of repression. The aftermath of Marcus's revolution, for example, is marked by instability and conflict, as different factions vie for power in the newly liberated society. The initial euphoria of liberation gives way to a period of uncertainty and repression, as the revolutionaries struggle to maintain order and establish a new social contract. This transition period is fraught with challenges, highlighting the complexity of rebellion's aftermath.

Moreover, individual acts of rebellion, such as Lena's, also encounter repression in the form of social ostracism and internal conflict. Lena's defiance of societal norms leads to her alienation from her family and community, illustrating how personal rebellion can result in isolation and psychological turmoil. Her journey reflects the broader theme that rebellion, while liberating in some respects, can also impose new forms of constraint and repression.

Character Development through Rebellion.

The characters in Chapter 7 undergo significant development as a result of their engagement with rebellion. Their experiences illustrate the transformative power of rebellion, as well as its potential to both liberate and repress.

1. Lena:

Lena's character arc is deeply intertwined with her acts of personal rebellion. Initially depicted as a compliant and submissive individual, Lena's rebellion marks a turning point in her development. Her defiance of familial and societal expectations is a catalyst for her growth, leading to greater self-awareness and autonomy. However, this liberation is accompanied by significant challenges, including social ostracism and emotional turmoil. Lena's journey highlights the dual nature of rebellion, as it empowers her to assert her identity while also exposing her to new forms of repression.

2. Marcus:

Marcus's character embodies the complexities of societal rebellion. As a revolutionary leader, Marcus is driven by a profound sense of justice and a desire to create a better society. His rebellion is both a political and moral crusade, aimed at dismantling an oppressive regime. While Marcus achieves significant victories, including the overthrow of the old order, his journey is also marked by personal sacrifice and moral ambiguity. The consequences of his rebellion reveal the inherent tensions between liberation and repression, as Marcus grapples with the unintended consequences of his actions.

Broader Implications for Society.

The exploration of rebellion in Chapter 7 also raises broader questions about the nature of society and the mechanisms of power. The narrative suggests that rebellion is an essential force for progress, yet it also underscores the need for careful consideration of its consequences.

1. Power Dynamics:

The interplay between rebellion and power dynamics is a recurring theme in the chapter. The overthrow of the old regime by Marcus's revolution illustrates how rebellion can shift power structures, creating both opportunities and challenges. The vacuum left by the old regime's collapse leads to a struggle for control, as different factions seek to assert their authority. This struggle highlights the fragility of liberation and the ease with which new forms of repression can emerge.

2. Social Change:

The chapter also explores the role of rebellion in driving social change. Lena's personal rebellion, while seemingly insignificant on a larger scale, represents the broader struggle for individual rights and self-expression. Marcus's revolutionary efforts, on the other hand, highlight the potential of collective action to bring about systemic change. Both forms of rebellion underscore the importance of challenging the status quo and the risks involved in doing so.

Chapter 7 of "Rebellion and Its Consequences" provides a nuanced exploration of how rebellion leads to both liberation and repression. Through the experiences of characters like Lena and Marcus, the narrative illustrates the transformative power of rebellion, as well as its inherent risks and complexities. The chapter's portrayal of rebellion as a multifaceted phenomenon, encompassing both personal and societal dimensions, offers a rich and insightful analysis of its consequences. Ultimately, the chapter suggests that while rebellion is essential for progress and change, it must be approached with a deep understanding of its potential to both liberate and repress.

Chapter 8: The Climax of Conformity

Examination of the climax involving McMurphy's fate

The climax of Ken Kesey's "One Flew Over the Cuckoo's Nest" occurs in the final section of the novel, specifically in Part 4, Chapter 4. This pivotal moment revolves around the fate of Randall P. McMurphy, the novel's rebellious and charismatic protagonist. The climax is a culmination of the ongoing struggle between McMurphy and the oppressive authority of the mental institution, embodied by Nurse Ratched. This examination will delve into the intricate layers of the climax, exploring its thematic significance, character development, and the broader implications for the narrative.

Setting the Stage for the Climax.

Before delving into the climax itself, it is essential to understand the context leading up to this moment. Throughout the novel, McMurphy has been a disruptive force within the institution, challenging the rigid rules and questioning the legitimacy of Nurse Ratched's authority. His actions are driven by a desire to empower his fellow patients, encouraging them to reclaim their individuality and autonomy. This rebellion reaches its zenith when McMurphy organizes a fishing trip, an act of defiance that further undermines Nurse Ratched's control.

The Climactic Event.

The climax of the novel is triggered by McMurphy's discovery of Chief Bromden's ability to speak and his decision to include Bromden in the fishing trip. This act of trust and camaraderie between the two characters symbolizes a deeper bond and mutual understanding. The fishing trip itself is a success, providing the patients with a sense of freedom and normalcy they had long been denied. However, the aftermath of this trip sets the stage for the climactic confrontation.

Upon their return to the institution, McMurphy and the patients are met with severe repercussions. Nurse Ratched, infuriated by McMurphy's continued defiance, decides to make an example of him. She subjects him to electroconvulsive therapy (ECT), a brutal and dehumanizing punishment. This treatment is meant to break McMurphy's spirit and serve as a warning to the other patients. The ECT scenes are harrowing, depicting the physical and psychological toll of Nurse Ratched's authoritarian regime.

Themes Explored in the Climax.

1. Power and Control.

The climax underscores the novel's central theme of power and control. Nurse Ratched's use of ECT against McMurphy is a stark representation of the institution's oppressive power. It highlights the extent to which those in authority are willing to go to maintain control over individuals who challenge the status quo. The ECT serves as a tool of intimidation, designed to suppress any further rebellion and reinforce the institution's hierarchy.

2. Resistance and Sacrifice.

McMurphy's fate in the climax is a testament to his unwavering resistance against conformity. Despite the physical and emotional pain inflicted upon him, McMurphy remains defiant. His willingness to endure suffering for the sake of his fellow patients elevates him to a heroic figure. This act of sacrifice is crucial in inspiring the other patients to continue their own struggles for freedom and self-expression.

3. Individual vs. Society.

The climax also explores the conflict between the individual and society. McMurphy's rebellion is not just against the institution but against societal norms that dictate conformity and obedience. His ultimate fate serves as a commentary on the price one pays for challenging societal structures and the courage required to stand up against oppressive systems.

Character Development.

McMurphy.

The climax marks a significant turning point in McMurphy's character arc. Initially introduced as a rebellious and somewhat self-serving figure, McMurphy evolves into a selfless leader who prioritizes the well-being of his fellow patients over his own safety. His decision to include Chief Bromden in the fishing trip and his stoic endurance of the ECT treatments reflect his growth as a character. McMurphy's transformation from a rebellious individual to a martyr-like figure underscores his role as a catalyst for change within the institution.

Nurse Ratched.

Nurse Ratched's character is also further developed during the climax. Her actions reveal the lengths she will go to maintain control and suppress dissent. The use of ECT against McMurphy exposes her cruelty and lack of empathy. This moment solidifies her role as the antagonist, highlighting her as a symbol of the dehumanizing and oppressive forces within the institution.

Chief Bromden.

Chief Bromden's character development is intricately tied to McMurphy's fate. Throughout the novel, Bromden is portrayed as a passive and voiceless figure, overshadowed by his mental illness and the institution's oppressive environment. McMurphy's trust and inclusion of Bromden in the fishing trip ignite a sense of empowerment within him. By the climax, Bromden begins to regain his voice and agency, setting the stage for his eventual escape and assertion of individuality.

The Aftermath and Its Impact.

The immediate aftermath of the climax sees McMurphy physically and mentally broken. His lobotomy, a result of Nurse Ratched's vindictive actions, leaves him in a vegetative state. This outcome is a poignant commentary on the destructive power of unchecked authority and the personal sacrifices made in the fight for freedom.

The impact of McMurphy's fate reverberates through the institution. The patients, particularly Chief Bromden, are profoundly affected by his sacrifice. Bromden's decision to smother McMurphy, ending his suffering, and subsequently escape from the institution symbolizes a final act of defiance and liberation. This ending underscores the novel's message about the resilience of the human spirit and the enduring fight for personal freedom.

The climax of "One Flew Over the Cuckoo's Nest" is a powerful and multifaceted moment that encapsulates the novel's central themes of power, resistance, and individuality. The climax not only resolves the narrative tension but also leaves a lasting impact on the characters and the readers, reinforcing the novel's enduring relevance and thematic depth.

The ultimate showdown between freedom and control

This chapter serves as the narrative climax where the protagonist's journey and the overarching conflict between individual autonomy and societal constraints are most intensely depicted. Through a meticulous examination of plot progression and character development, we can appreciate how this chapter encapsulates the essence of the struggle between freedom and control.

Plot Analysis.

Escalating Tension.

The chapter begins with a palpable escalation of tension. The protagonist, Alex, finds himself at the heart of a brewing rebellion against the authoritarian regime that has systematically suppressed individuality and freedom. As the resistance gains momentum, the regime tightens its grip, deploying increasingly draconian measures to quell dissent. This escalation is not merely a backdrop but a driving force that propels the narrative forward, highlighting the intensity of the conflict between freedom and control.

Key Events.

1. The Raid: The chapter opens with a raid on a clandestine meeting of the resistance. The regime's forces, using advanced surveillance technology, locate and ambush the rebels. This scene underscores the regime's pervasive control and the rebels' vulnerability.

2. Alex's Capture: During the raid, Alex is captured. His capture is a turning point, as it shifts the narrative focus from external rebellion to internal resistance. Confined and interrogated, Alex's resolve is tested as he faces psychological and physical torment.

3. Interrogation and Resistance: The interrogation scenes are crucial. They reveal the regime's methods of control, which include not only physical coercion but also psychological manipulation. Alex's resistance, despite the extreme duress, symbolizes the enduring human spirit's quest for freedom.

4. The Turning Point: A critical moment occurs when Alex, through sheer willpower, turns the tables on his interrogator. By exploiting a flaw in the interrogator's psychological tactics, Alex manages to sow doubt and discord within the ranks of the regime. This unexpected twist demonstrates the power of individual agency even in the most controlled environments.

5. Climactic Confrontation: The chapter culminates in a climactic confrontation between Alex and the regime's leader. This showdown is not

just a physical battle but a battle of ideologies. Alex, embodying the fight for freedom, challenges the leader's vision of a perfectly controlled society.

Character Development.

Alex: The Embodiment of Freedom.

Alex's character arc in this chapter is pivotal. Initially, he is portrayed as a reluctant hero, drawn into the resistance more by circumstance than by choice. However, as the story progresses, Alex evolves into a symbol of resistance. His captivity and subsequent defiance demonstrate his growth from a passive participant to an active agent of change. This transformation is underscored by his internal monologues, where he grapples with his fears and resolves to fight for his beliefs.

The Interrogator: A Proxy for Control.

The interrogator serves as a foil to Alex. Representing the regime's control, the interrogator is depicted as cold, calculating, and utterly devoted to the regime's ideology. Through the interrogator, the narrative explores the dehumanizing effects of absolute control. The interrogator's unwavering belief in the regime's doctrine highlights the dangers of blind conformity and the loss of individual moral responsibility.

The Regime Leader: The Architect of Control.

The regime leader, who appears briefly but significantly in this chapter, is portrayed as the ultimate embodiment of control. His character is crafted to be both charismatic and terrifying, embodying the seductive allure and the inherent danger of totalitarian power. The leader's interactions with Alex are charged with ideological tension, as each represents opposing worldviews.

Themes and Symbolism.

Freedom vs. Control.

The central theme of freedom versus control is vividly portrayed through the events and character interactions in this chapter. The raid and Alex's capture symbolize the regime's control, while Alex's resistance, both internal and external, represents the fight for freedom. The interrogation scenes delve into the psychological aspects of control, showcasing how authoritarian regimes manipulate and break individuals to maintain power.

Psychological Manipulation.

The regime's use of psychological manipulation is a critical element. The interrogator's tactics, which include inducing fear, uncertainty, and dependence, illustrate how control is maintained not just through physical force but through mental subjugation. This theme is further explored in Alex's internal struggle, where he battles not only his captors but also his own doubts and fears.

Symbolism of the Interrogation Room.

The interrogation room itself is a powerful symbol. It represents the regime's control apparatus and the extreme measures it employs to maintain dominance. The sterile, impersonal environment of the room reflects the cold, mechanistic nature of the regime's authority. Within this space, Alex's struggle becomes a microcosm of the larger fight for freedom.

Resolution and Implications.

Alex's Triumph.

The chapter concludes with a sense of cautious optimism. Alex's ability to outwit his interrogator and challenge the regime leader signifies a small but significant victory for freedom. This triumph, however, is not without cost. Alex's physical and psychological scars serve as a reminder of the harsh realities of resisting authoritarianism.

Broader Implications.

The resolution of this chapter sets the stage for the novel's final act. It leaves readers contemplating the broader implications of the struggle between freedom and control. While Alex's victory is a testament to the resilience of the human spirit, it also underscores the relentless nature of authoritarian regimes. The reader is left to ponder whether true freedom can ever be achieved in a world dominated by such powerful forces of control.

Through a gripping plot and nuanced character development, the chapter captures the intense struggle between individual autonomy and authoritarianism. Alex's journey from a reluctant rebel to a defiant hero exemplifies the enduring human spirit's quest for freedom, making this chapter a pivotal moment in the novel's narrative arc. The interplay between plot events and character arcs not only advances the story but also deepens the reader's understanding of the profound themes at the heart of the conflict.

The emotional and psychological toll on the characters

Key Characters and Their Emotional States.

Protagonist: Alex.

Alex, the central figure of the story, undergoes a significant transformation in this chapter. Initially introduced as a conformist who adheres strictly to societal norms, Alex begins to question the very fabric of his existence. This shift is catalyzed by a series of events that force him to confront the hollowness of his previously unexamined life.

Emotional Toll:

Alex's emotional journey is marked by a profound sense of alienation and disillusionment. As he starts to see through the façade of the society he once revered, he experiences a deep sense of betrayal. This betrayal isn't just against the society but against himself. The realization that he has been living a lie, conforming to expectations that stifled his true self, leads to intense feelings of guilt and regret. The weight of these emotions is palpable, manifesting in bouts of anxiety and depression.

Psychological Toll:

Psychologically, Alex's journey is one of self-discovery and painful introspection. The cognitive dissonance he experiences — the conflict between his ingrained beliefs and the new truths he uncovers — creates a mental turmoil that is both exhausting and enlightening. He grapples with questions of identity, purpose, and morality, leading to a profound existential crisis. The pressure to conform, which once seemed like a protective shield, now feels like a suffocating prison.

Antagonist: Mr. Harrison.

Mr. Harrison, the antagonist, represents the oppressive forces of conformity. As a high-ranking official in the societal hierarchy, he is the embodiment of the rigid structures that Alex is fighting against. His character is complex, driven by a mix of ambition and a genuine belief in the system he upholds.

Emotional Toll:

Mr. Harrison's emotional state is characterized by a sense of superiority and control. However, as Alex begins to challenge the status quo, Mr. Harrison's confidence starts to waver. The emotional toll on him is reflected in his increasing paranoia and insecurity. The once unshakeable belief in his own righteousness begins to crumble, replaced by a creeping fear of losing his power and status.

Psychological Toll:

Psychologically, Mr. Harrison experiences a significant shift. His previously clear-cut worldview becomes muddled as he is forced to confront the moral ambiguities of his actions. The psychological warfare between him and Alex becomes a battle for his own sanity. The pressure to maintain control in the face of mounting opposition strains his mental faculties, leading to moments of irrationality and erratic behavior.

Plot Development and Its Impact on Characters.

The Confrontation.

The climax of Chapter 8 is marked by a dramatic confrontation between Alex and Mr. Harrison. This showdown is not just a physical altercation but a battle of ideologies. Alex, armed with newfound knowledge and a burning desire for freedom, challenges Mr. Harrison's authority and the very foundations of their society.

Impact on Alex:

For Alex, this confrontation is a moment of catharsis. It is a release of pent-up frustration and anger, a defiant stand against the forces that have long oppressed him. The emotional intensity of this moment is overwhelming, as Alex finally voices the pain and disillusionment he has carried for so long. This confrontation serves as a turning point, solidifying his resolve to seek change.

Impact on Mr. Harrison:

For Mr. Harrison, the confrontation is a rude awakening. The psychological defenses he has built over the years begin to falter. The encounter with Alex forces him to question his own beliefs and the legitimacy of his power. This internal conflict is exacerbated by the realization that his once-unquestioning subordinates are starting to doubt him. The emotional distress of this realization manifests in a visible loss of composure, a stark contrast to his previously unflappable demeanor.

The Aftermath.

The aftermath of the confrontation leaves both characters deeply scarred. Alex, despite his triumph, is left with the burden of his newfound knowledge and the responsibility it brings. He is now a symbol of resistance, a role that comes with its own set of challenges and pressures.

Emotional Aftermath for Alex:

Emotionally, Alex is drained yet resolute. The initial euphoria of standing up to Mr. Harrison gives way to a sobering awareness of the uphill battle ahead. He grapples with the fear of failure and the potential repercussions of his actions. The support he receives from fellow dissenters provides some solace, but the emotional scars of his journey remain.

Psychological Aftermath for Alex:

Psychologically, Alex is more resilient. The confrontation has sharpened his mind, making him more adept at navigating the complexities of his new reality. He becomes more strategic in his thinking, understanding that the path to true change is long and arduous. The psychological scars, however, remain a constant reminder of the sacrifices made and the battles yet to be fought.

Emotional Aftermath for Mr. Harrison:

For Mr. Harrison, the emotional aftermath is one of humiliation and vulnerability. The loss of control and the exposure of his weaknesses leave him emotionally raw. The fear of retribution and the uncertainty of his future weigh heavily on his mind. This emotional turmoil leads to a profound sense of isolation, as he withdraws from those he once considered allies.

Psychological Aftermath for Mr. Harrison:

Psychologically, Mr. Harrison's world is shattered. The confrontation forces him to confront the limitations of his power and the fragility of his beliefs. He begins to question the very system he has dedicated his life to defending. This psychological upheaval leaves him vulnerable, a state that is foreign and unsettling to him. The once clear lines between right and wrong blur, leaving him in a state of existential confusion.

Themes and Symbolism.

The Climax of Conformity is rich with themes of identity, freedom, and resistance. The emotional and psychological toll on the characters serves as a microcosm of the broader societal issues explored in the novel.

Identity and Conformity:

The struggle between individuality and conformity is a central theme. Alex's journey symbolizes the internal conflict faced by individuals in a conformist society. The emotional and psychological toll of this struggle highlights the cost of sacrificing one's true self for the sake of societal acceptance.

Freedom and Oppression:

The confrontation between Alex and Mr. Harrison encapsulates the broader theme of freedom versus oppression. The emotional intensity of their battle reflects the stakes involved in the fight for personal and societal liberation. The psychological impact on both characters underscores the devastating effects of oppressive systems on the human psyche.

Resistance and Change:

The chapter also explores the theme of resistance and the courage required to challenge the status quo. Alex's emotional and psychological journey is a testament to the transformative power of resistance. The toll it takes on him is a reminder of the sacrifices necessary for meaningful change.

I skillfully portrays the emotional and psychological toll of conformity on the characters, using their journeys to explore broader societal themes. Alex's transformation from a conformist to a rebel and Mr. Harrison's descent into insecurity and doubt are both poignant and thought-provoking. The chapter leaves a lasting impression, highlighting the profound impact of societal pressures on the human spirit and the courage required to break free from them.

In summary, the emotional and psychological toll on the characters in Chapter 8 is a central element of the narrative. It is through their struggles and transformations that the novel's themes are brought to life, offering a powerful commentary on the human condition and the quest for individuality in a conformist world.

Chapter 9: The Aftermath of Freedom

Reflection on the outcomes of the rebellion

This chapter serves as a crucial pivot, reflecting on the outcomes of the characters' struggle for autonomy and the broader implications for the society in which they live.

Plot Analysis: The Consequences of Rebellion.

The immediate aftermath of the rebellion is marked by a mix of chaos and cautious hope. The rebellion, initially driven by the quest for freedom and equality, has left the society in a state of flux. Structures of power have been shaken, and the void left by the deposed authority creates an environment ripe for both opportunity and peril.

Political Turmoil and Power Vacuum.

In the wake of the rebellion, the old regime has been dismantled, leading to a significant power vacuum. This vacuum becomes a battleground for various factions seeking to establish dominance. The struggle for power is characterized by shifting alliances and betrayals, reflecting the uncertainty of the new era. The narrative explores how different groups vie for control, each driven by their own visions of what the post-rebellion society should look like. This struggle highlights the complexities of revolution; while the old order has been overthrown, the path to a new order is fraught with challenges.

Social Reconstruction and Identity Crisis.

The rebellion also triggers a profound social reconstruction. Characters who were once oppressed now find themselves in positions of power, grappling with the responsibilities and expectations that come with it. This shift is not without its internal conflicts. Many characters experience an identity crisis as they transition from resistance fighters to leaders and lawmakers. The novel delves into their psychological turmoil as they navigate their new roles and the weight of the expectations placed upon them.

Economic Shifts and Inequality.

The economic landscape undergoes significant changes as well. The redistribution of resources and wealth is a contentious issue, with former elites stripped of their assets and the new regime attempting to implement more equitable systems. However, this process is not smooth. The novel illustrates the difficulties in achieving economic justice while avoiding the pitfalls of corruption and inefficiency. The struggle to balance fairness with pragmatism becomes a central theme, highlighting the tension between idealism and reality.

Character Development: The Evolution of Protagonists and Antagonists.

Protagonists: From Revolutionaries to Leaders.

The protagonists of the story undergo significant development in this chapter. Having achieved their goal of overthrowing the oppressive regime, they are now faced with the task of rebuilding society. Their evolution from revolutionaries to leaders is marked by both triumphs and setbacks.

Protagonist A: Initially a fierce fighter driven by a personal vendetta, Protagonist A now seeks to establish a just and fair society. Their journey is one of self-discovery as they learn the complexities of governance and the necessity of compromise. This evolution is portrayed through their interactions with former enemies and allies, revealing a more nuanced and mature character.

Protagonist B: Contrasting with Protagonist A, Protagonist B struggles with the burden of leadership. Their idealism is tested as they confront the harsh realities of power. The narrative explores their internal conflict, questioning whether the ends justify the means and whether the new order truly represents the ideals for which they fought.

Antagonists: Adapting to the New Order.

The antagonists also experience significant character arcs. Those who were once in power must now adapt to their diminished status, leading to varied responses.

Antagonist A: This character represents the old guard, clinging to the remnants of the past. Their resistance to change and attempts to undermine the new regime highlight the persistence of old prejudices and power dynamics. Their arc serves as a reminder of the enduring influence of the old regime and the difficulty of achieving lasting change.

Antagonist B: In a surprising twist, Antagonist B undergoes a transformation, becoming a reluctant ally of the new regime. Their journey from antagonist to ally is marked by moments of redemption and self-reflection. This transformation adds depth to the narrative, illustrating that change can come from unexpected quarters and that redemption is possible even for those who once opposed the rebellion.

Themes and Symbolism: The Price of Freedom.

Chapter 9 is rich with themes and symbolism, reflecting the multifaceted nature of freedom and its costs.

The Price of Freedom.

The central theme of this chapter is the price of freedom. The characters' struggle for liberation comes at a great cost, both personally and collectively. The narrative explores the sacrifices made and the losses endured in the pursuit of a better society. This theme is poignantly depicted through the characters' reflections on their journey and the toll it has taken on them.

The Symbolism of Rebirth.

The aftermath of the rebellion is also a period of rebirth. The destruction of the old order symbolizes the potential for new beginnings. This rebirth is fraught with challenges, but it also represents hope and the possibility of creating a more just society. The novel uses imagery of renewal and growth to convey this theme, emphasizing the cyclical nature of history and the opportunity to build anew.

Reflection on the Outcomes of the Rebellion.

The reflection on the outcomes of the rebellion is a pivotal aspect of Chapter 9. The narrative prompts readers to consider the broader implications of the characters' actions and the nature of revolution itself.

Mixed Outcomes.

The outcomes of the rebellion are mixed, reflecting the complexity of real-world revolutions. While there are significant gains in terms of freedom and equality, there are also considerable losses and challenges. The novel does not shy away from depicting the harsh realities and the unintended consequences of the rebellion. This balanced portrayal adds depth to the story, encouraging readers to think critically about the nature of change and the difficulties of achieving it.

Lessons Learned.

Through the characters' experiences, the novel imparts important lessons about the nature of power, leadership, and the human condition. It underscores the idea that the fight for freedom is ongoing and that the struggle does not end with the overthrow of an oppressive regime. The characters' journeys highlight the need for vigilance, adaptability, and a commitment to justice, even in the face of adversity.

The characters are left to grapple with the consequences of their actions and the new reality they have created. The narrative does not offer easy answers but instead invites readers to engage with the complexities of revolution and its aftermath. Through its nuanced portrayal of the outcomes of the rebellion, the novel provides a rich and thought-provoking exploration of the themes of freedom, power, and the enduring quest for justice.

In summary, Chapter 9 of the book offers a profound reflection on the outcomes of the rebellion, delving into the political, social, and economic ramifications while exploring the evolution of its characters. The chapter's rich thematic content and symbolic depth make it a pivotal part of the story, encouraging readers to contemplate the true cost of freedom and the challenges of building a new world from the ashes of the old.

Chief Bromden's journey towards self-empowerment

Ken Kesey's One Flew Over the Cuckoo's Nest is a seminal work that delves into themes of power, control, and individuality within the oppressive confines of a mental institution. Central to this narrative is the character of Chief Bromden, a Native American patient who embarks on a profound journey of self-empowerment. Chapter 9, "The Aftermath of Freedom," is pivotal in this context, marking a significant turning point in Bromden's development. This analysis will explore Bromden's evolution towards self-empowerment, focusing on the narrative and character development within this chapter.

Setting the Stage: Bromden's Background and Initial State.

Chief Bromden, the novel's narrator, is introduced as a seemingly mute and towering figure, marginalized not only by his mental illness but also by his ethnic background. His narrative is interwoven with hallucinations and a deep sense of paranoia, reflecting his perception of the world as a mechanized system designed to oppress individuals. This "Combine," as

Bromden calls it, represents the oppressive forces of society that seek to strip people of their autonomy and individuality.

At the beginning of the novel, Bromden is a passive observer, his sense of self eroded by years of institutionalization and his identity suppressed by the dehumanizing environment of the mental ward. His journey towards empowerment begins subtly, catalyzed by the arrival of Randle P. McMurphy, a boisterous and rebellious patient who challenges the authority of Nurse Ratched and the institution's rigid control.

The Role of McMurphy in Bromden's Empowerment.

McMurphy's influence on Bromden is profound. McMurphy's defiance and charisma awaken something within Bromden, sparking a desire for freedom and self-assertion. The chapter opens in the aftermath of a dramatic confrontation between McMurphy and Nurse Ratched, a clash that symbolizes the broader struggle between individual autonomy and institutional control.

McMurphy's act of rebellion—breaking the glass window of the nurse's station—serves as a catalyst for Bromden's transformation. This act of defiance, though seemingly minor, is monumental within the context of the ward's oppressive regime. It signifies a breach in the seemingly impenetrable control of the Combine, and for Bromden, it represents a glimmer of hope and possibility.

Bromden's Internal Struggle and Awakening.

He reflects on his past, his father's downfall, and the loss of his cultural identity, all of which contribute to his sense of powerlessness. This introspection is crucial for understanding Bromden's journey. The memories of his father, a once-proud chief who was broken by the white society, mirror Bromden's own feelings of inadequacy and defeat. However, McMurphy's influence begins to shift Bromden's perspective, encouraging him to reclaim his sense of self.

Bromden's awakening is also marked by his increasing awareness of his physical capabilities. Throughout the novel, Bromden's size and strength are emphasized, yet he often feels small and powerless due to his mental state and the oppressive environment. In this chapter, Bromden starts to recognize his physical presence as a source of potential power. This realization is a critical step in his journey towards empowerment.

Symbolism and Imagery in Chapter 9.

Kesey employs rich symbolism and imagery to convey Bromden's transformation. The imagery of machinery and fog, which Bromden uses to describe his perception of the world, begins to change in this chapter. The fog, which represents his mental fog and the dehumanizing fogging machine of the Combine, starts to lift as Bromden becomes more aware and assertive. This shift in imagery signifies Bromden's growing clarity and determination.

The symbolism of the glass window, broken by McMurphy, also carries significant weight. Glass, a fragile and transparent barrier, symbolizes the invisible yet potent forces of control exerted by the Combine. By breaking the glass, McMurphy shatters not only a physical barrier but also a symbolic one, demonstrating to Bromden that the Combine's power is not absolute. This act empowers Bromden, showing him that resistance is possible and that he too can break free from the constraints imposed on him.

Key Events and Turning Points in Chapter 9.

1. McMurphy's Rebellion: The chapter begins with the aftermath of McMurphy's act of rebellion. The broken glass window and the subsequent reactions of the staff and patients highlight the disruption of the ward's routine and the challenge to Nurse Ratched's authority. Bromden observes these events with a mixture of awe and fear, recognizing the power of defiance.

2. Bromden's Reflections: As Bromden reflects on his past and the stories of his father, he begins to connect his personal struggle with the

broader theme of societal oppression. This introspection is crucial for his development, as it allows him to understand the root of his feelings of powerlessness and to see a path towards reclaiming his identity.

3. Interactions with McMurphy: Bromden's interactions with McMurphy in this chapter are marked by a growing sense of camaraderie and mutual understanding. McMurphy's encouragement and belief in Bromden help to bolster his confidence and self-worth. These interactions are pivotal in Bromden's journey, as they provide him with the support and inspiration he needs to begin asserting himself.

4. The Lift of the Fog: Towards the end of the chapter, Bromden experiences a moment of clarity, symbolized by the lifting of the fog. This moment represents a significant shift in his mental state, as he begins to see the world more clearly and to recognize his own potential for action and change.

Bromden's Empowerment: A Gradual Process.

Bromden's journey towards self-empowerment is gradual and fraught with challenges. Chapter 9 is a critical juncture in this journey, but it is not the culmination. Instead, it marks the beginning of Bromden's active participation in his own liberation. His growing awareness and assertiveness set the stage for his eventual rebellion against the Combine.

Throughout the novel, Bromden's empowerment is portrayed as a complex and multifaceted process. It involves not only his recognition of the oppressive forces at work but also his willingness to confront and challenge those forces. McMurphy's influence is crucial, but Bromden's journey is ultimately his own. He must navigate his internal struggles and external obstacles to achieve true empowerment.

Through the influence of McMurphy, the rich symbolism and imagery, and Bromden's internal struggles and reflections, Kesey crafts a narrative that highlights the transformative power of resistance and the potential for individuals to reclaim their autonomy in the face of oppression. Bromden's evolution from a passive observer to an empowered individual is a testament to the resilience of the human spirit and the enduring quest for freedom and self-determination.

The lasting impact of McMurphy's legacy on the other patients

In Ken Kesey's novel One Flew Over the Cuckoo's Nest, Chief Bromden's character serves as a catalyst for change within the mental institution. Chief Bromden's legacy is a complex tapestry woven through the lives of the other patients, fundamentally altering their perceptions of freedom, self-worth, and rebellion against oppressive systems. Chief Bromden's influence is most profoundly felt in the aftermath of his dramatic and tragic end, leaving an indelible mark on the ward's inhabitants.

The Awakening of Individual Identity.

Chief Bromden's presence and actions awaken a sense of individual identity among the patients, who initially appear as mere extensions of the institution's dehumanizing machinery. His rebellious spirit and overt defiance against Nurse Ratched's authoritarian rule ignite a spark of resistance in the other patients. For instance, Chief Bromden, who starts as a seemingly mute and powerless figure, finds his voice and strength through his interactions with Chief Bromden. The transformation of Chief Bromden from a passive observer to an active participant in his own life is a testament to Chief Bromden's lasting impact.

Chief Bromden's assertion of individuality is mirrored in other patients as well. The once timid and compliant individuals begin to exhibit signs of self-awareness and autonomy. This awakening is a direct result of Chief Bromden's encouragement to question the oppressive regime and reclaim their identities. By challenging the institution's power dynamics, Chief

Bromden empowers the patients to see themselves as more than just their diagnoses, fostering a sense of dignity and self-respect.

The Theme of Rebellion and Resistance.

Chief Bromden's legacy is deeply rooted in the theme of rebellion and resistance. His defiance against the institution's rigid control mechanisms inspires the other patients to resist in their own ways. This rebellion is not always overt but manifests in subtle acts of defiance that collectively undermine the institution's authority. For example, the patients begin to engage in small acts of disobedience, such as speaking out against Nurse Ratched or refusing to adhere strictly to the ward's rules.

Cheswick's rebellion is a poignant example of Chief Bromden's influence. Cheswick, who initially appears as a meek and compliant patient, becomes emboldened by Chief Bromden's fearless demeanor. His eventual act of defiance, although tragic, underscores the ripple effect of Chief Bromden's legacy. Cheswick's rebellion, albeit short-lived, signifies a break from the oppressive conformity imposed by the institution, highlighting the transformative power of Chief Bromden's influence.

The Impact on Chief Bromden.

Chief Bromden's legacy has a particularly profound impact on Chief Bromden, whose narrative perspective frames the story. Chief Bromden's journey from a seemingly deaf and mute patient to a narrator who reclaims his voice and agency is one of the novel's most compelling arcs. Chief Bromden's interactions with Chief Bromden serve as a catalyst for this transformation. Chief Bromden's unwavering belief in Chief Bromden's potential and his encouragement to confront his fears play a crucial role in Chief Bromden's eventual liberation.

Chief Bromden's final act of breaking through the window and escaping the institution symbolizes his liberation from the mental and physical confines that had entrapped him. This act of defiance, inspired by

Chief Bromden's legacy, signifies Chief Bromden's reclaiming of his identity and freedom. Chief Bromden's escape represents the ultimate triumph of individual will over institutional oppression, a theme central to Chief Bromden's character arc.

The Transformation of the Ward's Dynamics.

Chief Bromden's impact extends beyond individual transformations to alter the overall dynamics of the ward. His presence disrupts the established order, creating fissures in Nurse Ratched's authoritarian rule. The patients, who once lived in constant fear and subjugation, begin to assert themselves, challenging the institution's control. This shift in power dynamics is a direct consequence of Chief Bromden's rebellious spirit and his ability to inspire others to resist.

The ward's environment, characterized by strict routines and oppressive control, gradually becomes a space where patients feel empowered to express themselves. Chief Bromden's legacy fosters a sense of community and solidarity among the patients, who begin to support each other in their collective struggle against the institution. This camaraderie is a stark contrast to the isolation and competition that Nurse Ratched had cultivated to maintain control.

The Symbolic Significance of Chief Bromden's Actions.

Chief Bromden's actions throughout the novel carry significant symbolic weight, contributing to his lasting legacy. His decision to undergo electroshock therapy despite knowing its debilitating effects is an act of sacrifice that underscores his commitment to challenging the institution's authority. This sacrifice elevates Chief Bromden to a martyr-like figure, whose legacy continues to inspire the patients even after his death.

Chief Bromden's tragic end, resulting from his physical confrontation with Nurse Ratched's orderlies, further cements his legacy as a symbol of resistance. His death, though brutal, serves as a powerful reminder of the costs of rebellion and the necessity of fighting against oppressive systems. The patients' reaction to Chief Bromden's death, marked by a mixture of grief and defiance, highlights the profound impact he had on their lives.

The Psychological Liberation of the Patients.

Chief Bromden's legacy is also reflected in the psychological liberation of the patients. His unwavering belief in their potential and his encouragement to confront their fears play a crucial role in their psychological healing. The patients, who initially appear as mere shells of their former selves, begin to exhibit signs of psychological growth and resilience.

Chief Bromden's insistence on the patients' inherent worth and his refusal to accept their dehumanizing treatment by the institution foster a sense of hope and possibility. This psychological liberation is evident in the patients' increased self-esteem and their willingness to confront their inner demons. Chief Bromden's legacy, therefore, transcends physical liberation, encompassing a deeper, more profound impact on the patients' mental and emotional well-being.

The Role of Humor and Camaraderie.

Chief Bromden's use of humor and camaraderie as tools of resistance leaves a lasting impact on the patients. His ability to find joy and laughter in the face of adversity provides a stark contrast to the institution's grim and oppressive atmosphere. This humor serves as a coping mechanism, enabling the patients to endure the harsh realities of their confinement.

The camaraderie fostered by Chief Bromden's presence creates a sense of solidarity among the patients. They begin to see themselves as part of a collective, united in their struggle against the institution's control. This sense of community is a direct result of Chief Bromden's influence, highlighting the transformative power of shared resistance and mutual support.

The Legacy of Empowerment.

Chief Bromden's legacy is ultimately one of empowerment. His influence empowers the patients to reclaim their identities, assert their individuality, and resist oppressive systems. This empowerment is a testament to Chief Bromden's enduring impact, which transcends the confines of the institution and resonates on a deeper, more universal level.

The patients' journey towards empowerment is marked by their increased self-awareness, resilience, and willingness to challenge the status quo. Chief Bromden's legacy serves as a beacon of hope, inspiring the patients to envision a future beyond the confines of the institution. This legacy of empowerment is Chief Bromden's most enduring contribution, reflecting his unwavering belief in the inherent potential of each individual.

Chief Bromden's legacy in One Flew Over the Cuckoo's Nest is a multifaceted and enduring influence that fundamentally alters the lives of the other patients. His rebellious spirit, commitment to individual freedom, and unwavering belief in the patients' potential leave an indelible mark on the ward's inhabitants. Chief Bromden's impact is evident in the patients' awakening of individual identity, their acts of rebellion and resistance, and their psychological liberation.

Through his actions and sacrifices, Chief Bromden becomes a symbol of resistance and empowerment, inspiring the patients to reclaim their identities and challenge the oppressive systems that seek to control them. Chief Bromden's legacy, therefore, transcends his physical presence, leaving a lasting imprint on the patients' lives and underscoring the novel's central themes of freedom, individuality, and the human spirit's resilience.

Printed in Great Britain
by Amazon